the house in the waves

Martin has spent most of his fourteen years in foster homes and institutions, but for much of the time he has lived in a secret world of his own, deep inside himself, where the seagulls on the wall are his closest friends and where nothing outside can hurt or frighten him.

Concerned that the boy is losing all contact with reality, his doctor arranges for Martin to go to Carisburgh, a special home near the shore, for expert care. But in the course of treatment Martin seems to be slipping further and further away.

Then a strange balloon—skin-colored and with the following message stuffed inside starts Martin on an extraordinary episode:

> Hee who findes this may finde mee a prisoner
> against my wille atte the Senechal's Howse
> in Carisburgh. Mine uncles madnesse daily
> grows—I fear for my lyfe. Helpe me if you
> have a harte for I cannot helpe myselfe.
>   Wille Howlett

Martin is transported to old Carisburgh, a bustling city not yet destroyed by the raging sea. There he is pitted against a violent storm as well as the half-mad alchemist who holds young Will prisoner in the Senechal's House— the house in the waves.

Martin himself has been the prisoner of his own mind, and this strikingly unusual story juxtaposes vivid psychological reality with the most stirring fantasy and adventure. It is a novel that may be read on many levels and one that will hold the interest of readers of all ages.

the house

in the waves

JAMES HAMILTON-PATERSON

S. G. PHILLIPS   *New York*

For Thomas Wordsworth,
with love

the house in the waves

1

Dr. Smedley was hairy—tufts of brownish bristles grew out of each nostril and a black lawn flourished on the back of each hand. At least once a week for the last two years Martin had sat in the same easy chair in Dr. Smedley's room and gazed at the backs of the doctor's hands. From the first the hairs had repelled him, and as if Martin were in free fall in a kind of emotional outer space, with nothing to hinder movement, the initial impetus of his repulsion had set him drifting farther and farther away from the doctor. Week by week, the distance growing between them was hardly perceptible, but over the span of months Dr. Smedley had indeed grown smaller and smaller so that by now he had dwindled to a dot. Only his voice refused to go away.

"Martin, you must try to listen to what I'm saying. You're losing contact again. You must make more effort."

Deep inside Martin felt a sigh heave itself but he couldn't speak. How often had he heard Dr. Smedley say the same words? In not answering he wasn't deliberately being rude; it was simply that the words no longer meant anything to him. Once, Martin remembered, he had gone to a school. He couldn't be sure how long ago it was, but he had vague memories of morning assemblies at which everybody had to repeat things called prayers, meaningless jumbles of sound that the boys reeled off like the multiplication tables. Nobody had ever explained to him quite what they were for, but he assumed they had to be learned as part of what were called "tests." He had therefore memorized them without difficulty and filed them away in his mind. Similarly, Martin had paid attention to Dr. Smedley's words at first. As week after week the doctor had said the same meaningless things, Martin had reasonably imagined he was repeating something like prayers, something that might be needed later in a test. He had filed them away accordingly.

"You're back in that world of your own," Dr. Smedley was saying. Automatically, Martin's mind supplied the end to this well-known catechism.

" 'You may think it's the real world'," he said inwardly to himself, " 'but the real world is outside, the world of people and sunshine and animals.' "

"You may think it's the real world," echoed Dr. Smedley's voice, "but the real world is outside. That's the world of people and sunshine and animals. *I'm* in the real world," he added as a sort of amen.

On days like this Martin would find his own way from the room in which he slept down through warm corridors filled with silent children in bathrobes, who glided like fish among the artificial glades of an aquarium, down to Dr. Smedley's real world. This was a room that had been carefully furnished so as to avoid any suggestion of a doctor's consulting room. There wasn't even a desk in it, merely a couple of easy chairs half turned to face an electric fire set in the wall and a bookcase full of old magazines with half a bottle of whiskey on top. For as long as Martin could remember this bottle had been half full; he had once wondered if the "whiskey" were nothing but a thin coat of paint inside an empty bottle like the imitation pints of milk he had once been expected to play with.

Martin sat in his armchair and in the other, five feet away, sat the little blob that had once been Dr. Smedley. The blob was speaking, making a disproportionate amount of noise, but Martin could no longer follow the words. Instead, his eyes were fixed on the wallpaper. This was a particularly airy design of sea gulls—again, carefully chosen—and attracted him as much as Dr. Smedley's hairiness repelled him. Martin had grown very friendly with the sea gulls. All the time he was in the room, which he knew perfectly well was a consulting room, he would watch the gulls floating across the walls, wheeling around the chromium square of the electric fire, calling to each other. Sometimes they sounded happy and Martin envied them being safely together within the four blue walls of this warm room. At other times their cries were sad and Martin knew it was because they were trapped inside forever, when all the time they longed to be free to fly where they liked over an endless blue sea. Martin had never seen the sea, but of its blueness and endlessness he had never been in doubt; the very word had become a synonym for freedom.

"Tell me what you're thinking," said the dot in the chair opposite suddenly. Martin made a huge effort.

"I was listening to the sea gulls," he said, twisting his head to look at each wall in turn as the birds swooped and soared.

"Not again, Martin?" said Dr. Smedley despairingly. "I thought we'd been over that last time. Don't you remember? You agreed that the gulls aren't real birds at all—they're just pictures on the wallpaper. Go on, touch them again if you won't believe me."

Slowly, lovingly, Martin stretched out a thin hand which he passed gently over the wall nearest him.

"Well?" queried Dr. Smedley, with a hint of impatience.

"They're there," said Martin in a small voice. "I can feel them . . . *inside,* sort of."

"Oh, Martin . . ." The doctor's voice frayed away into silence as if worn out by the boy's insistence.

"You think I'm making it up," said Martin defensively.

"No, no. No, of course I believe you. But don't you remember a single thing we talked about last week?"

The boy and the doctor gazed at each other, each from his own world.

"We'd better go over it again," said Dr. Smedley at length, trying to keep his voice bright. "You can tell me everything about the gulls—I know you're telling the truth, Martin. Come on, we know each other well enough by now."

Martin looked away.

"I saw the shells again last night," he said. His voice was so soft that Dr. Smedley had to lean forward to hear the words. "They were crying because I was leaving them to die and I couldn't explain to them . . . they didn't know they were going to be buried for millions of years. I couldn't tell them."

"Martin, you mustn't——." But whatever it was he ought not to do was left unspecified, for at that moment there was a knock on the door and a young man in a white coat looked in. "Will you excuse me a minute, Martin?" Dr. Smedley said, standing up. "I'll only be a second." He went out, leaving the door slightly open, and stood talking to the young man in the corridor.

Martin paid him no attention; he was remembering last night's dream, still vivid in his mind. It had been the result of a curious episode. About ten days previously he had been allowed out for his usual walk around the grounds. Near the kitchens, a series of grimy sheds with lead drainpipes that steamed perpetually, some excavations were being made for the foundation of a new wing. The noise of machinery had drawn Martin over to the pit that had once been a threadbare lawn. At the bottom of the pit a bright yellow bulldozer nosed around, making snarling lunges at the ochre earth. The engine revved and died alternately, sending black jets of diesel fumes straight up in exclamation points. Martin, standing on the crumbling edge, watched the monster's hot groveling for a long time. Painted on the side of the machine in capital letters was the word DROTT; the name seemed to him to suit perfectly the sound and activity of the bulldozer. At length the driver pulled the knob that released the compression and the engine hissed to a halt. In the silence that followed Martin picked his way down the slope to the bottom of the pit where bunches of workmen stood about. One of the men spotted him.

"You can't come down here, son," he called. "Nobody's allowed on the site."

Martin couldn't/wouldn't hear. He walked with his hands in his pockets and his head bent to the bulldozer, which still gave off quivers of heat, the engine ticking as it cooled. He moved silently all around it, noting the dusty glass carburetion telltale full of pink fuel, the thick silver pistons, which disappeared up the greasy steel sleeves, and how they controlled the elevation of the scoop in front, and the caterpillar tracks that were clogged with mud and smashed bricks. Everything was on such a huge scale. Martin, accustomed to a way of life that encompassed neat chromium gadgets and clinical instruments, was awed by the way whole rocks lay ignored and harmless as grit in the giant molars of the driving gear.

"Here, come on, lad." The man had followed him around. "It's dangerous on a site and we're not insured for unauthorized personnel." It sounded like something he had learned by heart, a workman's prayer.

Again Martin seemed not to notice. He was picking at a fragment of sandstone wedged in the lip of the scoop. It came loose suddenly and Martin was holding in the palm of his hand a perfect seashell. It was a bivalve, the two halves seemingly cemented together into a pinkish, heart-shaped pebble.

"Where did this come from?" asked Martin. The man stepped closer to look.

"Dunno," he said. "Could've come anywhere out of this lot." He indicated the excavation with a vague gesture.

"But this is a seashell," said Martin, "and there isn't any sea near here."

"That's a fossil, that is," said the workman, whose buddies were now gathering around to see what was going on. "There's lots of them here."

"That's right," said a stringy man with a red helmet. "Millions of years old, they are. Look," and he led Martin over to the level area that the bulldozer had just been clearing. Set in the sandstone floor like tangerine segments in a jelly were hundreds of shells all jumbled together. Some were in bunches, some lay singly; some were whole, others were smashed. The bulldozer had scored white mounds across this ancient graveyard.

"Used to be under the sea, this place did," explained the stringy man. "But that's enough, son," he added. "You heard Ted here—sites is dangerous. We'll all get the dickens if you're seen down here." He put out an arm as if Martin were a sheep to be herded away from a precipice.

Still Martin didn't hear the words. He was standing on the seabed holding his shell while the warm prehistoric water swished around his ankles. The excavation site had become a lagoon; beyond it, the institution had crumbled into the future and in its place was an open waste of waves, a seething broth of rudimentary life. For a million years Martin stood there, the water ebbing away from around his feet while betrayed creatures flopped and strangled in the diminishing pools. Soon the last moisture dried, the beach cracked painfully like winter-slit lips, and Martin could see only a fissured wasteland studded with the shells abandoned by the sea and left to die.

Deep in this dream Martin had been steered away from the site by the scrawny man as the bulldozer turned in its sleep, coughed, and roared into his consciousness. Since that afternoon Martin had gone to bed with the shell beneath his pillow; by day he carried it with him as if such tenderness might atone for the terrible indifference of history. Now, as he sat in Dr. Smedley's deep chair, Martin remembered the recurrent dream that had returned once again the previous night. In the dream he had become the sea in which the shells had fed and lived. A huge, wild mother, outwardly rough but soft and nourishing underneath, he had cared for the shells and all the living creatures that depended on him and loved him in return. But one day he felt himself being dragged away from his children. It was as if an arm had been put around his waist from behind and was pulling him backward. When they felt his withdrawal the shells had cried out, their lips parting in horror, their tongues blackening and shriveling inside. Martin had cried, too, pounding the shore with his green fists as he receded, trying to explain that he couldn't help his betrayal, his voice growing ever fainter as he poured out his grief. At this point Martin always awoke in the arms of the night nurse, his face wet with tears, choking on his love for the dead creatures whose trust he had betrayed.

Martin could see Dr. Smedley standing outside in the corridor still talking to the young man in the white coat.

"I must go, Philip," the young man was saying. "I haven't finished my rounds yet and I have to pop up to Building Three to see the Bancroft girl. She was fifteen a couple of days ago."

"Bancroft? Bancroft?" puzzled Dr. Smedley's

voice. "Oh yes, she's the one about halfway down on the left, isn't she? Wish her a happy birthday for me."

"Good heavens," exclaimed the young man, "she's not that much with it, she hasn't a clue about birthdays. It could be Christmas for all she knows."

The two men outside chuckled. Martin was hunched in misery on his chair as Dr. Smedley came back into the room and pushed the door shut with his heel.

"Sorry about that diversion," he remarked. "Now, where were we? Oh yes, your seashells. Well, look, Martin, it does no good to feel sorry for *things*, does it? You should try to feel sorry for people instead." He looked earnestly at the thin, dark child who huddled opposite, hugging his strange world to himself.

"I don't know any people," the boy finally whispered.

"Nonsense," said Dr. Smedley jovially, "of course you do. What about all your friends here? What about Miranda? What about me?"

Martin thought of Miranda, a merry blonde girl who came from the town to help with the cleaning. She had just had her seventeenth birthday. One day when she had been working in his room, she had asked him to her party, but Martin hadn't been sure he wanted to go. Over the previous month he had felt something intangible coming between Miranda and himself. Something was different about her. She no longer gave him her undivided attention, no longer sat on the edge of his bed and shared giggly confidences whose secrecy Martin respected with all the love that was in him. She had changed. In any event, Martin had drawn back into himself so far that he wasn't allowed to travel across town to her party. Which was just as well, as it turned out, for at the party Miranda had announced her engagement to a young man who drove a milk-truck. Since then Martin had stared out of the window with his back to her while she dusted and swept and chattered her happiness. There were no more confidences, no more secrets; her kisses and hugs seemed cursory and meant for somebody else. Now Martin's nightmares of betrayal became more vivid, more devastating.

"I don't know any people," he repeated almost inaudibly.

Dr. Smedley looked at him consideringly, his head slightly on one side. Martin stared back, noticed the nasal hairs fluttering as the doctor breathed, looked away abruptly and glared at the wall to his right. The sea gulls started to move, their faint cries growing more and more strident. Martin listened, absorbed and full of a pity he couldn't express. The gulls were unhappy, he knew that. They no longer wheeled sedately in the blue security of Dr. Smedley's room. They were trying to escape, battering themselves against the walls to find a way out of their prison. Their only urge was to freedom and their cries became louder and more frustrated as Martin sat immobile, deafened by their screams and stunned by their beating wings.

Unnoticed by the boy, Dr. Smedley was watching him all the while, his head still on one side. He saw a pale, skinny boy with dark hair staring fixedly at the wall. It was hard to imagine he was fourteen; his body was that of a young child. Dr. Smedley was not fooled, however; two years' acquaintance with Martin had impressed on him the singularly adult way in which the boy was acutely sensitive to people's motivation and he guarded himself accordingly. In two years Dr. Smedley had learned practically nothing about Martin. Not only that, but sometimes the doctor had the uncomfortable suspicion that Martin had learned all there was to know about him. Now Martin's periods of withdrawal were becoming more frequent and more prolonged. A turning point had obviously been reached.

In his mind, Dr. Smedley briefly reviewed the case. The green file he had inherited when Martin first became his patient contained a mass of notes and a newspaper clipping, dated some eight years previously, which he now knew by heart:

> Cyril Molloney, 30 years old, an electrician, of Bottle St., appeared today in Bow Street Court charged with the willful neglect of his son, Martin, age 6. The boy was found wandering three days ago by a policeman who said that when

found, Martin was in "a shocking condition, miserable and half-starved." He had been taken to Mercy Hospital and was now making satisfactory progress.

In court today a welfare official testified that Martin had a year's history of almost complete absenteeism from school. The boy was committed to the Child Care Officer as being in urgent need of care and attention.

In a statement the father said: "I couldn't do a thing with him; he has been like a wild animal lately. Sometimes he won't even speak to me. It doesn't seem to make any difference hitting him." Molloney was ordered to be bound over pending a psychiatrist's report. His wife, Doreen, died last year.

The case notes in the file further related that Martin had been removed from his disturbed environment when he was six and that during the next half-dozen years he had been in and out of schools and foster homes, continually running away and being found roaming the streets, lost and alienated. At last, when he was spending only a few days in each new institution before escaping, there had been a court order and he had been "permanently referred for treatment." Too many police hunts had been launched, too many search parties hastily convened, too many ice-bound canals dragged by frogmen. Patience had run out.

As Dr. Smedley watched the boy something like genuine pity moved him through his layer of professionalism, like a magnet influencing iron filings through a pane of glass. For eight years this undersized creature had lived a lonely and impersonal existence in institutions, shuttled from one to another with nothing but a suitcase and a folder of case notes to his name. But he, obviously, was not getting anywhere with the boy. Some other step must be taken. It was, of course, against the rules of the game to deceive a patient, but Dr. Smedley always sought, and usually found, the easiest way. The time had come for a break.

"You must have a holiday, Martin," he said in a kindly voice. "You deserve a change."

There was no answer. Martin was with his gulls.

"You must believe me, I do want to help; we all do," Dr. Smedley added with something approaching truthfulness.

He watched in the empty quiet of the room as Martin sat perfectly still, his face turned to the wall—only the glint of tears on his thin cheeks betrayed his silent weeping.

During the next week Dr. Smedley accordingly set in motion the buff-colored machinery that would make good his vague promise. Martin was enamored of the sea, evidently, so he would be sent to the sea. Council notified council; telephones were picked up in green, tea-stained offices;

psychiatrists' reports were initialed; transportation was arranged.

"You *are* lucky," said Miranda to Martin one morning in what she hoped was an envious voice. "Being sent to the seaside. Golly, I wish somebody would send me away on a holiday," she lied cheerfully, thinking how unbearable it was to be even a mile away from her milkman fiancé. Oh well, she reflected, the poor child wouldn't understand *that*. She had grown quite fond of him and his pinched little face, she supposed. And he certainly seemed to have taken a shine to her; not that he had a clue as to what it was all about, of course . . . Oh Alan, she thought, remembering the arms made strong by heaving milk crates at dawn; oh Alan.

Martin stood at his window as usual, looking unseeingly out at the site of the excavation. In one pocket his hand played with the fossil shell he had found. Although they all talked of his having a holiday and "taking a break," he realized that it was just another way of saying that he was to be passed on to someone else. Not that he liked this place especially, but in two years he had become accustomed to it, and in such loveless circumstances familiarity passed easily for real affection. Martin knew he would not be coming back again. As he tried to visualize what he would miss most, he was only too aware that the next place might well be indistinguishable. There would be the same warm corridors, the same consulting suites masquerading in mufti as private sitting rooms, the same avuncular doctors. Even now he couldn't evoke a clear image of Dr. Smedley: the hirsute man had shrunk too far into an anonymous pinpoint. But Miranda . . . the window blurred suddenly and he sniffed. She was so *comforting*—and in any case Martin hardly ever spoke to anyone else. The other children of his own age were either hopelessly retarded (Stuart was a sweet, hulking teen-age infant) or unapproachable in their delinquent ferocity.

Behind Martin, Miranda had finished. She paused at the door with the wastebasket in one hand, the greasy incense of floor polish filling the room like her personal scent.

"Bye, love," she said. "I'll see you before you go—promise me, now." She smiled reassuringly.

"I'm not coming back, am I?" asked Martin, still looking out of the window. His breath made gray mist on the glass.

"Why ever not?" demanded Miranda.

" 'Cause I've been transferred," said Martin simply.

"They'd have told me," said Miranda.

Notice how she says neither yes nor no, Martin told himself. The situation was clear. They had decided that they could no longer cope. In a sudden panic of loss Martin swung around, but Miranda had gone. He was left leaning against the sill trying not to cry, his fist balled around the seashell, thinking of the new dimension this gave his dream. His complicity accused him: now he was deserting even his gulls.

2

THE NEXT DAY they transferred Martin in a Ford minibus to his new home. With him in the back of the van traveled a matronly woman and all his belongings, which somehow fitted easily into a single suitcase. At the beginning of the long journey the woman made comforting remarks to Martin, at first even trying to draw him into conversation. But Martin, even though he had anticipated his removal, was still too shocked by his sudden uprooting to respond and her efforts dwindled to occasional injunctions to "look at the cows" and similar fatuities. Eventually she abandoned her good intentions and slid along the cold plastic bench until she could lean on the back of the front seat by the driver. They covered the best part of the journey like this, Martin sitting alone in the rear of the bus, the two adults up front, discussing the cost of living.

They drove eastward to Suffolk until the driver

said that they were now only a mile from the sea. Martin awoke at this remark and peered out of the window, but because there were no hills to provide a vantage point the sea remained invisible and there was nothing to indicate where the flat, wet landscape finally gave up and sank wearily under the waves. Soon the bus slowed down and turned in at a drive. On one gatepost a wooden plaque announced CARISBURGH HALL. PRIVATE. Unconsciously, Martin's eyes searched for and found the high iron fence he had expected to see hidden in the laurel jungle on either side of the main gate. It gave him no feeling of extra security.

Martin's new home turned out to be a solidly built Victorian mansion. A gray woman wearing a lead medal gave them a subdued welcome. His belongings, his green file, and finally Martin himself were all handed over, together with the opinions of the matronly woman who had accompanied him on the journey.

"We're all awfully sorry to lose him," she said to the gray woman in what she imagined was a confidential whisper. "Martin's a sweet boy, really. But he's just not *there* most of the time, you know? Oh, and you have to be quite careful about his baths. He likes privacy, the funny boy, but he *will* forget to dry himself." She laughed a gurgly, comfortable laugh, like a hot-water bottle being shaken.

The gray woman seemed immune to her confidential humor.

"It's most kind of you," she said, "but we do

have quite a bit of experience here at Carisburgh Hall." She pronounced it "Caresborough," the first syllable a long bleat and the last half of the word brusquely clipped. It sounded like a sergeant's bellow followed by a regiment's boots crunching to attention. Much intimidated, the other woman backed away to the bus with a fixed smile of appeasement on her face, remembering only at the last moment to dart back to Martin and give him a quick farewell hug before retreating once more. Martin turned away and looked up at the lights of the institution that were just coming on as dusk fell. Behind him the minibus doors slammed, the engine started, and the crunching tires receded down the drive.

"You poor boy," said the gray woman, putting an arm around his waist, "what a welcome for you after coming all that way."

Martin was steered through the heavy porch and into a brightly lit hall; at one end a giant stone fireplace was surrounded by a half-dozen over-stuffed armchairs of the type in which businessmen with veined noses snooze off their heavy lunches. Piles of creased magazines lay about, mostly appealing to those thinking of themselves as country gentry, full of glossy pictures of hounds and tweedy ladies. It was evidently a place in which much waiting had to be done.

"My name's Miss Brunt," the gray woman was saying, "and I'll try to be as much help to you as you want me to be." Her grimness seemed to have dissolved with the bus's departure and she chattered on while they climbed the main staircase together past a window set with the stained-glass figure of a woman holding a lily. "Now, we'll just dump your things and then whiz off and have some tea. I expect you're famished." Her cool eyes observed the thin boy beside her with professional competence, saw the way he was holding himself stiff with defensiveness, not daring to relax or move more than was necessary, like someone gingerly lowering himself into a scalding bath.

From deep inside himself Martin was peering cautiously out at his new surroundings, the broad staircase and the chattering stranger who led him up it. He searched desperately for something familiar but found nothing. In one pocket his hand clenched harder around the fossil shell.

Upstairs, the décor changed. The hallway and the front stairs could have been those of a faded country club but on the first floor the institution began. The smell of antiseptic and furniture polish, the food carts pushed back against the wall, the half-open doors on either side revealing white beds or stacked wicker laundry baskets that creaked as unseen hands flopped folded linen into them. Miss Brunt opened a door and ushered Martin inside. The room was warm and had thick curtains already drawn against the raw September evening. There were two beds in it and on one side of them Miss Brunt dropped Martin's suitcase.

"Yours," she said. "Not uncomfortable, either: I slept in it myself once for three nights. We're a bit pushed for space at the moment, I'm afraid,

28

so I hope you don't mind sharing. I've put you in with Ropey Dunning now that Charlie's . . . er . . . gone on a holiday. Ropey's a jolly sort, but you'll find that you're quite a bit *older* than he is, so do be nice to him."

Martin walked over to the window and held one of the curtains back. Dusk made a black mirror of the glass and all he could see was his own outline and behind him the figure of Miss Brunt with the light bulb blazing above her head. He thought of Miranda and the privacy of his old room.

"It's awful, I know, being moved about like this," said Miss Brunt sympathetically, gently turning him away from the window with one hand and closing the curtains behind with the other. "It's completely upsetting. I always take at least a week to get used to anywhere, which is why I never go to a strange place for my vacation. I mean, it's just not worth it, is it? A whole week gone out of a scant two weeks. Let's go and have some tea."

They went into the corridor and returned the way they had come, Miss Brunt talking continuously to the silent boy at her side.

"You know what they do to cats when they have to go to a new home, don't you? They smear butter on their paws. Cats, of course, like their paws absolutely clean, so the first thing the wretched cat does is to sit down and try to lick the butter off. The idea is, I believe, that if there's a lot of butter all over its feet, by the time the poor

29

thing gets it off it will have become accustomed to its new surroundings. Though personally," said Miss Brunt practically, "I can't think why one shouldn't use margarine. It's much cheaper and I don't imagine a cat could tell the difference."

She chatted on like this all the way down the stairs and along another corridor. Finally, she stopped in front of a large oak door through which sounded the rattle of cutlery and the heavy clatter of thick china.

"Here we are," said Miss Brunt. "Don't worry. I'll sit next to you." She opened the door.

Inside there were several long tables and, against one wall, a vast sideboard laden with Pisas of plates and saucers. There was also a tea urn with a faucet that dripped gray tea onto a dishcloth spread on the floor beneath. Around the tables in the middle was an assortment of chairs and benches on which sat Martin's new companions. Some of the children were eating, others were being fed by patient-looking nurses. In one corner of the room squatted a girl of about ten with a jam-smeared plate on her head. She was singing loudly and happily but no one paid her any attention. Miss Brunt nodded to some of the staff and sat down at the head of one of the tables. She patted the end of the bench on her right.

"You go here," she said. "I hope you like tea?" When Martin didn't answer she called over one of the green-uniformed maids who patrolled with metal teapots. "Two, please, Kitty," she said. "Nice and milky for this young man, I should think. His name's Martin and he's just come to join us."

Kitty was a red-faced, cheerful woman in her forties. As Martin was still standing, tensely holding on to the edge of the table with one hand, she leaned her motherly weight on his shoulders and he slid stiffly down onto the bench.

"Hello, Martin," she said. "Nice to have you with us."

"This is Martin, everybody," said Miss Brunt, raising her voice and beaming. All the staff and one or two of the children looked up.

"Hello, Martin."

"Hello."

" 'Lo."

The little girl in the corner stopped singing, gravely took the plate off her head, as if she were an elderly minister greeting a parishioner, and smashed it on the floor beside her. Then she went on singing again, a high wordless song that floated up to the ceiling and hung above the general clatter.

"Janice is at it again," one of the green uniforms said.

Martin saw all this from within himself but felt nothing. None of it had anything to do with him. He was not aware that Miss Brunt fed him a jelly sandwich and a cupcake and held his mug for him, nor was he conscious of the curious stares some of the other children gave him. He was back with his shells in the prehistoric ocean of his dream, lulled by the warm waves that rocked him gently in a timeless cradle. The ground swell of the lagoon rolled him luxuriously about the seabed, like a peppermint ball in the mouth of a fat schoolboy, and he lolled and tumbled in an ecstasy of security among the familiar teeth of rock. On another plane of reality Martin's face was wiped and Miss Brunt escorted him from the dining room to a room like Dr. Smedley's. A bald young man sat in a deep armchair reading the case notes from the green file.

"This is Martin, Doctor," said Miss Brunt. "He's just had his tea. I think he still feels a bit strange here, as you might expect."

"How are you, old man?" asked the young doctor but Martin was a million years away, happily curled up on the seabed. The young man consulted his notes once more. "'Complete withdrawal,'" he read aloud. "Well, Nurse Brunt, that's certainly what it looks like from here. Has he said much?"

"Not a word, Doctor."

"Perhaps it's just shock. We'd better make sure he gets a good night. I suggest half an hour in the television room and then bed. I'll prescribe a sedative. A couple of hundred milligrams should do it. We don't want him groggy tomorrow."

"Very well, Doctor."

Miss Brunt led Martin away and into another room. A handful of children were watching television with varying amounts of attention, presided over by a nurse whose tired eyes missed nothing of what her charges were doing. But the bright screen never came within Martin's field of vision. He was seeing, instead, glittering, swaying plankton and wandering diatoms, their geometric fragility outlined like microscopic snowflakes. All around him were trees of seaweed with rubber trunks, whose fronds waved up towards the surface, and ragged outcrops of coral shot through by the silver bullets of tiny fish. Martin wasn't actively conscious of any one of these things: he was only aware of them all together as forming a world in which he was entirely safe. They were simply the visual counterpart to the song the water sang in his ears, long, warm chords that held him peacefully suspended. It was a world in which he had always belonged—and always would.

Somewhere, another Martin was helped to his feet, given a pill, quickly bathed, and put into bed. An hour later when Miss Brunt came in with his roommate, Ropey Dunning, Martin was sound asleep. As she helped undress Ropey Miss Brunt looked curiously and with pity at the unconscious boy who had moved at her side like a sleepwalker through Carisburgh's evening corridors. She had seen them come and seen them go, talking voluble nonsense or unable even to move; she had seen fits and tantrums, wild tears and laughter with no apparent cause; but she could never remember a child who had seen so much around him but had deliberately not noticed it, who had clearly heard most of what people said to him but purposely kept silent. She felt more hopeful about Martin

33

than she had about any of her patients for a long time.

Ropey Dunning's fat buttocks trembled as he knelt on his bed unraveling a sock. They were the first thing Martin saw on opening his eyes the next morning. He felt heavy and wrenched, as if he had been dredged up from the ocean floor.

"If you still feel a bit sleepy, don't worry," said Miss Brunt when she came in some minutes later. "We gave you a pill last night to make you sleep, didn't we? Remember?"

Martin rolled his head negatively on the pillow.

"Oh dear, Ropey, that *is* a mess," sighed Miss Brunt after she had drawn back the curtains. She sat on the end of his bed and tried to gather up the yards of gray wool that lay springily on the blankets. The fat boy, who was probably about twelve, lay on his stomach with an end of wool in his mouth and pounded his feet on the pillow, a huge grin opening his face.

"I haven't got all the time in the world, you know, Ropey," went on Miss Brunt. "It isn't as if I haven't enough to do without picking up after you." Ropey giggled. "We're very short staffed, you see," added Miss Brunt, presumably more to herself.

The truth of this was amply demonstrated during Martin's first month at Carisburgh Hall. He gradually unfurled in the warmth of his new surroundings, like a tight bud timidly wondering whether spring was just a confidence trick. He was

shown kindness everywhere, but with the insight
that Dr. Smedley had observed, he was also aware
that because the staff members were always so
rushed the kindness had had to be built into the
curriculum, as it were, rather than permitted to
happen spontaneously. There simply wasn't the
time for everybody to be attended to equally.
Many of the children required intensive supervision, and when the nurses weren't having to offici-
ate at regular events, such as meals and bedtime,
they were bustling up and down the corridors from
one minor calamity to another. C753621 CO. SCHOOLS

There were about forty children being looked
after at Carisburgh and within the first two weeks
their faces had become part of Martin's everyday
scenery. If he had ever had any plans for friendship at the back of his mind, however, he soon
abandoned them. Most of the children were like
those at his previous institution: too retarded or
too wild for the sort of friendship he needed; and
because Carisburgh was reserved for those cases
that people like Dr. Smedley had failed to cope
with, they tended to be more retarded and even
wilder. Martin's roommate, Ropey Dunning, came
the nearest to being a suitable companion. True,
he had infantile lapses and strange episodes of
amazing ferocity, but often he would show an
adequate grasp of what went on around him. However, his understanding was limited to those things
that he could touch and see. One day after lunch
both boys were lying on their beds for the com-
pulsory rest period when Martin suddenly found

that he needed to talk to someone. In his brief, hesitant way he told Ropey about his personal world where the sea lulled you to sleep and about the gulls trying to escape from a distant room because they wanted to fly freely over the sea. At last he showed Ropey his fossil shell. The fat boy examined it minutely, then popped it into his mouth. But because it wouldn't crunch or taste of raspberries, he spat it out on the floor and then began to wail uncontrollably.

Martin's expression changed immediately. He retrieved his shell, wiped the spit off it, and put it lovingly back into his pocket. At this moment the door opened.

"Why, Ropey, whatever is the matter?" asked Miss Brunt as she bustled into the room. "Come, come. Calm down, now, and stop making such a fuss. It can't be that bad." Ropey's sobs softened to liquid hiccups. "Now, what's this all about?" Miss Brunt looked inquiringly at Martin, who had gone over to the window and was staring out.

"I was telling him about the world," said Martin in a hurt voice.

"Silly world," gulped Ropey, his cheeks inflamed.

"It's not."

"It is."

"Not."

"Is."

"Now, now, you two," broke in Miss Brunt, "that's enough of that."

It was not only enough for Miss Brunt; it was

enough for Martin as well. He was now thoroughly convinced of the stupidity of throwing open his private world to the public, like some impoverished peer; the public merely trampled all over it, apparently trying to ruin it out of spite. In the future he would allow nobody in; it was as simple as that. The bald young doctor, whose name was Dr. Herbert, made only a little more effort than Dr. Smedley had done to get over the threshold. At first Martin had seen him as a new face, but after the face had made the same old expressions and had opened to say the same old things as Dr. Smedley, Martin lost interest and it started receding into the distance. Nowadays Dr. Herbert was about the size of a golf ball. Only Miss Brunt remained anything like life-size.

"Please try," Dr. Herbert kept saying. "Please try to come out of yourself, Martin. You'll be quite safe."

Martin, of course, knew better. After all, for his sea creatures to leave their shells meant certain death; there were far too many predators around to risk venturing out in all one's nakedness. He would gaze around the pink-washed walls of the doctor's room, missing his gulls terribly, although he knew they weren't far away. He had only to close his eyes to be deafened by their screaming.

"Martin, listen to me," begged Dr. Herbert. "There are people here who love you."

"Ssh," whispered the sea in the boy's ear, "*you don't have to believe that. He doesn't know what love means.*"

"No," said Martin aloud. "Everything I want's inside me."

"But there are plenty of people outside who care a lot about you. Miss Brunt, for one." Beneath the level of his desk top Dr. Herbert glanced discreetly at his watch. The rumble of the alarm clock in his stomach had just woken him up to the fact that it was nearly lunchtime.

"Miss Brunt's nice to everybody," said Martin. "You all are. That's your job." Then he went back to the sea, trying to explain to all his friends that he wasn't deserting them, that they were far more real and important to him than bald Dr. Herbert.

"Dear Martin," called the gulls, *"we know we are."* And the shells sighed, *"We love you, we love you. Don't ever leave us."*

"I never shall," promised Martin.

To provide the maximum inducement for Martin to leave his inner world, the experts at Carisburgh Hall planned plenty of interesting allurements in the way of lessons. Martin's education had been patchy. When he had actually been in school, in between his prolonged wanderings on the loose, he had learned a fair amount. He picked up information without difficulty; his only problem lay in relating it to the world in which he lived. He could read and write: communication had seemed important even if there were nobody he wished to communicate with. Equations and French irregular verbs, on the other hand, he memorized as he had morning prayers. They were all apparently nonsensical but they had come in handy for tests. From some time before his arrival at Carisburgh, however, he had been having fewer and fewer lessons because he was too withdrawn to learn anything. Much daunted by his total silence and occasional weeping fits, his teachers had lost all their enthusiasm. It was like lecturing to an empty hall; sooner or later they realized that they were merely addressing themselves and that, of course, was pointless. An even greater silence had descended upon Martin.

Now, however, new-style lessons were arranged. These were made as varied and exciting as possible in the hope of cajoling him back into life again. Several of the younger occupational therapists would sit with him in turn in a quiet corner of a large room on the top floor. Other children were being urged to paint, make models, weave or act playlets, but Martin, having proved immune to the charms of these diversions, was tempted with appetizing titbits of science and succulent snippets of history. Many of the other boys learned how to use lathes and drills in the workshop, but because Martin evinced not the least interest in practical skills the most he ever did was perform elementary chemical experiments. The nurses were dedicated but soon dampened by his refusal to participate with any enthusiasm. He was given illustrated books to back up what he had been taught about local history, geography, and the universe. There were pictures of the damage the sea had caused to the East Anglian coastline within a few miles of where he sat, portraits of primitive villages in Borneo, photographs of lunar craters. The only time he betrayed a slight gleam of curiosity was in biology, when the organisms that live in the sea were discussed; but the gleam short-lived, quickly extinguished, as if Martin were afraid it might shed too much light on the world inside him.

In desperation, Miss Brunt hit on the idea of appealing to his sense of fantasy by telling him stories. She would sit on his bed after she had gone off duty and, straining her imagination to the utmost, she would retell all the Hans Christian Andersen and Grimm stories she could remember, trying to transpose them into modern times. It was quite a feat and would leave her with a wrung-out feeling that invariably required an early bed-time. Mostly she would get no reaction at all from Martin. She watched him as she talked, a thin, dark child lying on his back staring blankly at the ceiling. When she finished she would kiss his forehead, tuck him in, and say good-night. Martin never answered her; it was difficult to tell whether he had even heard, but Miss Brunt, apparently, was clearly convinced that he had, because she persisted stoically in the face of his seeming indifference.

The question of Martin's freedom arose from the start. During the first week it seemed as if he were never going to be allowed to leave the building, and the old trapped feeling came over him. The days went by in a gloomy indoor succession: meals, lessons, rest periods, more meals, and then sessions with Dr. Herbert.

"Nice to have plenty to do," remarked the doctor. "There's nothing so depressing as boredom."

"You're buttering my paws," said Martin sullenly, but the significance was quite lost on Dr. Herbert. *Makes incongruous remarks,* he wrote in the green folder in front of him. *Still identifies with animals.*

It was Miss Brunt who perceived how restless Martin was becoming and she interceded for him.

"He's not a fool, Doctor," she told the bald young man one day. "He knows he's being kept in until he's properly settled, because we're scared he'll run away. Any day now he'll try to escape."

Miss Brunt put her case well. She pointed out that the grounds of Carisburgh Hall were extensive and that he could hardly come to much harm in them. "Anyway," she said, "unless somebody starts treating him as a responsible human being, he'll never learn how to be one, will he?"

Young Dr. Herbert found her practical, experienced approach intensely aggravating, mostly because he knew she was right. He resented very much being told his job by a gray, middle-aged woman, even if it was only by implication.

"What she needs is a husband," he told himself and discovered that this made him feel better. He then waited a discreet couple of days before suggesting that Martin be allowed out.

Martin, cheered into one of his less indrawn moods, gave his solemn promise, as he had done in the past, not to run away. And, as he had done in the past, he ran away.

The day was fine and mild. He walked across the fields behind the ponderous building until it was out of sight, hidden by a gaunt, leafless copse. On all sides stretched the flat countryside. An enormous emotion welled up in him, a huge desire to escape. He hated the institution; he hated the kind, impartial people, the hopeless children, the dullness. Without being really conscious of having made a decision, Martin found himself pushing through heavy laurel boughs, climbing the high iron fence, and dropping into the road beyond. His restlessness had to be appeased; he was not just escaping *from* somewhere, he was escaping *to* something, something that had been calling him like a friend.

"Kept asking where the sea was," said the woman with glass cherries on her hat who brought him back to Miss Brunt, "so I knew he was a stranger hereabouts. One of the Hall's poor darlings, I shouldn't wonder, was what I said to myself. Looked so lost, the dear lamb. Is there any hope for him, Nurse?"

"Any hope that he's in time for tea, you mean?" demanded Miss Brunt with a swift return to her military manner. "Of course there is; we only started five minutes ago." She took Martin's arm tenderly. "Many thanks," she threw gruffly over her shoulder as she led him off to the dining room, leaving his captor standing uncertainly among the bulbous armchairs in the hallway.

Nobody was angry. In fact, Dr. Herbert seemed obscurely pleased.

"Off again, were you, old man?" he said and nodded. "I'm not surprised; it's quite a habit you have. We really ought to see what we can do about breaking it."

Threatened and miserable, Martin withdrew immediately into his inner refuge. He went back to his sea dreams, and the screaming nightmares returned with increased ferocity. Late each night the nurse on duty held him tightly, with the light on to bring him back, wet with tears, from his undersea dreams of betraying his friends, the shells. He never spoke. He had to be clothed, fed, and bathed. The outside world became a mad blur of images. It was sometimes as if he were alone in a snow-covered valley and suddenly saw an avalanche starting down the side of a mountain toward him, getting faster and bigger, swallowing everything in its path. The nearer it got, the less able he was to move out of its way. Soon he could see it was composed of a wild mixture of red-brick buildings and people in white coats and carried with it a moraine of unrelated facts about oxygen and the Battle of Hastings and fish gills. Just before he was engulfed completely he saw, precariously balanced on top of the mass, a Gothic castle with a girl in a white dress leaning out of a topmost window about to be rescued by an armored knight whose sword dripped with boiling dragon's blood.

"I think we'll start with a spot of narcosis," observed Dr. Herbert. "Everything's getting a bit too much for the boy. He needs a rest. Would you arrange a change of bed, please, Nurse?"

"Certainly, Doctor," said Miss Brunt.

"I mean, he's not assimilating a thing like that, is he?" Dr. Herbert nodded toward Martin who sat rigid and apparently unconscious.

Perhaps something did get through to him; maybe only the serious tone of what was said rather than the words themselves. Temporarily shocked out of his stupor into a passive obedience, Martin persuaded Miss Brunt, a few days later, to let him out for some fresh air. He walked, trembling, down the short flight of stone steps outside that led to the fields behind the house. The steps seemed to stretch on and on in a white blur while the sky hummed, but at last he was down. He knew now that he would always be like this—a whole lifetime of Dr. Herberts and Dr. Smedleys stretched before him. Tears ran into the corners of his mouth.

3

MARTIN WASN'T SURE when he first saw the balloon. He had been wandering about the grounds of the estate, watching the sea gulls drawing crooked circles in the sky and feeling the tug of the sea pulling his feet toward a distant beach. Suddenly he was aware of a milky blob the size of a football hanging in the air about a hundred yards away, and as soon as he saw it he knew it was important. As he broke into a run a gust of wind caught the blob and blew it into the branches of a nearby tree. From underneath Martin could see that it was wedged, like a stray moon, about twenty feet up. He began to climb.

Having lived in a world of tiled corridors and gritty patches of city grass, Martin was not adept at tree climbing. However, with a good deal of scrabbling he forced himself up in a crackle of snapped twigs and finally arrived, breathless and much scratched, at the place where the thing had stuck. Swinging a leg over a stout branch he sat precariously and examined the balloon. It seemed to be made of semitransparent paper, very thin and tough and so tautly blown up that his fingers pattered hollowly on it. Martin saw that not only was it about the same size as a football but it was made like one, too, out of many small panels stitched minutely together. At the bottom there was a little crimped nozzle, like the tied-off end of a German sausage, and from this dangled a thin tube of paper about as big as a cigarette and sealed with a blob of scarlet wax.

Martin realized that he would have to get both himself and the balloon back to earth before he could investigate further; it was already difficult enough ensuring that he didn't fall out of the tree without the added problem of letting go of his handholds to examine the balloon. After a moment's thought he gripped the nozzle between his teeth, letting the roll of paper hang down over his chin and the balloon float up in front of his face like a giant piece of bubble gum. Then he cautiously began to climb down again.

It was not easy. Each time Martin looked down for a foothold the balloon floated over his eyes, bouncing softly on the end of his nose. Gradually, though, he found it easier to see and by the time his feet touched the ground he was congratulating himself on his technique for descending trees while carrying a balloon between the teeth. It was only then he discovered the descent had become easier largely because all the time he had been going down the balloon had as well. He took it out of his mouth and looked at it. It lay in his hands, denting and crinkling as the air leaked out through a split seam. At last it fell in upon itself, still light and so translucent that Martin could see the outline of his hands through its papery skin. Gently, he laid it on the grass and carefully untied the paper tube from its neck. Then he broke the seal and unrolled it. The first thing he noticed was that it wasn't paper at all but the same thin material the balloon was made of, and the second was that the message was written very beautifully, like the examples in a book on handwriting he had once had to copy from.

Hee who findes this may finde mee
a prisoner agaynst my wille
atte the Seneschal's Howse
in Carisburgh. Mine uncles madnesse
daily grows—I feare for my lyfe.
Helpe mee if you have a harte
for I cannot helpe myselfe—
Will Howlett

Martin read this aloud several times, struggling a bit with the unfamiliar spelling. Overhead the gulls soared and called; inside, Martin's heart bumped. From which direction had the balloon come? The wind was blowing off the sea, bringing with it hungry gulls; it must also have brought the balloon. Martin stood facing the wind, clutching the message to himself. Somewhere ahead, he knew, was the sea that had been calling to him for so long. In the same direction was also the prisoner who had written to him. Martin had no doubt that he was intended to get the letter—it wasn't accidental. The balloon had come with the white gulls from the sea, and everything that came from the sea spoke directly to Martin. His eyes filled with tears of gratitude. It was actually the first letter he had received in his entire life.

In a moment or two he became unaccustomedly practical. He sensed that the afternoon was half-over—if he stayed out much longer they would come looking for him. It was most important that he should be allowed to continue the freedom his parole had given him, and if he were accused of running away again Dr. Herbert might recommend that he be no longer let out by himself. It sometimes seemed to Martin that from the time he was first able to toddle he had been chased by people as if they were park-keepers running after a piece of wind-blown litter with a spiked stick. With loud cries he would be accused of untrustworthiness by complete strangers who hadn't even spoken to him, much less trusted him; then he would be deposited somewhere convenient, tidied away, and forgotten about.

But now, he knew, there would be no reckless truancy for him—this message was too important to be put at risk. He must go back and make his plans for getting away without arousing suspicion; Will Howlett was depending on him. Martin folded up the note and put it in his inside pocket. Then he carefully rolled up the limp tissue bladder that only ten minutes before had been floating proudly over Suffolk and put that in his pocket as well. With a last look around to make sure that there was no more evidence of this extraordinary event other than the scatter of broken twigs under the tree he had climbed, he walked back across the fields to the Hall.

It was one of those autumnal afternoons that smell of wet rooks. Clouds were coming up from the North Sea with the early moon but the sky overhead was still bald and blue. High, high above the fields and the gulls a brilliant vapor trail was slicing the sky neatly in two. Nine miles high and fifty miles long, the white wound drew itself from a gleaming knifepoint, slowly healing as the freezing high-altitude winds made ragged scar tissue, which then blew away into nothing. After the aircraft had disappeared Martin watched the last of the slit become a furrow, the furrow a frayed ribbon, the ribbon tatter into grains and strands and wisps before vanishing altogether behind the black roofs of the Hall. His new happiness allowed him to be very moved.

Martin was careful not to let his excitement betray him. At teatime he allowed himself to be helped to tea and doughnuts in his usual impassive silence, but today he could afford to notice the dining room and its occupants without having to hide away in his deep-sea world. It was as if a volcanic island had suddenly heaved itself up and burst through the surface; from this firm vantage point he could now survey his surroundings with a strange confidence. He could even feel sorry for the other children who didn't know about the real world outside Carisburgh Hall, much less have a friend in it. Little Janice was sitting in her usual corner, singing away as she bored a hole through her bun with one finger. Ropey Dunning sat on the luxurious cushions of his bottom, his shorts stretched like sausage skins and the insides of his legs chafed red as chapped cheeks. Poor Ropey, thought Martin, remembering how the fat boy had tried to eat the seashell. Now Ropey grinned happily as he crammed his mouth with dough, jam leaking between his fingers, grains of sugar stuck on the underside of his nose.

All this Martin noticed while the plates emptied succulent bun one of Ropey's pudgy fingers set out and the tables became geographical with gray lakes of tea, pale islands of margarine, gritty deserts of sugar. While his mouth coped valiantly with its on an arduous voyage through this land, trudging through deserts and paddling over lakes, pausing only to smear a greasy isthmus across a pond before sallying on to the crumbly foothills of a mountain range of discarded crusts. Then Miss Brunt suddenly stood up, hands and faces were wiped, and a dishcloth was dropped into the middle of the tabletop world.

In his habitual silence Martin suffered being shepherded into the T.V. room, and while the children's programs prattled on, he lay on the carpet, gazing up at the flickering ceiling and puzzling about Will Howlett. Why should his uncle keep him a prisoner, even if he were mad? When should a rescue attempt be made? Martin decided that some time during the night he must try to find some food to take with him, for he was determined to find the town of Carisburgh the next day and if possible to locate Will. While he was planning, his hands kept patting his pockets, his ears listening for the crackle of the note and balloon he had found.

Within half an hour Martin was taken to his bath. Bath nights went by schedule and tonight happened to be his turn. There were several bathrooms dotted about the building, some with a single tub and others with two. Because Martin disliked bathing with anyone else he was usually allotted a single bath and Miss Brunt limited her supervision to keeping a discreet eye on him, presumably to ensure that he didn't drown. Tonight, however, owing to a noisome defect in the plumbing, his usual bath could not be used. It was a huge old-fashioned affair with brass taps like fire hydrants and a plunger, which had WASTE printed on the top, instead of a plug. Martin was rather fond of this bath, but when they got upstairs they found three inches of gray water in the bottom of the tub and a terrible smell of musty drains. Martin was transferred to one of the bright new double bathrooms, which had been installed in what used to be a parlormaid's room. He was inwardly so confident and cheerful that he wasn't much depressed by this; even the sight of Ropey Dunning being soaped in the other tub was not enough to threaten his mood. He sat up with his chin on his knees and let the water become absolutely still so that only his breath dimpled the surface. Then he opened one of his hands and let his fossil shell plop and wobble down to the bottom where it lay on the white enamel. This was a ritual he performed without fail every bath night; it was the least he could do to make amends for having taken the shell out of its deep bed and away from its companions. After a million years of being locked in the middle of a slab of sandstone it could once more lie under soft, warm water and lurch gently in the eddies set up when Martin moved his toes.

But the ceremony wasn't casting its usual spell. For the first time Martin's thoughts were not for his shell alone; his mind kept straying to Will Howlett and the balloon. Eight feet away Ropey wallowed like a pink whale, snorting with pleasure. Sometimes he lunged about in the water, chasing the soap, but often he would stand up in the bath and trudge around. Ropey's tight blubber glistened a bright salmon color, thin lines of deeper red under his chest and around his waist marking the creases he folded into when sitting down. Miss Brunt wore a loose-fitting rubber apron that did little to protect her as she tried to restrain the splashing, yelling boy. Finally some soap found its way into one of Ropey's eyes and he stopped charging about long enough to wail and jam his fist into it. Only then could Miss Brunt get some sort of grip on his slippery acres of flesh.

Against the background of all this noise and steam Martin evolved his plan. Sometime during the night he would creep downstairs and steal some food and then tomorrow he would set off to find Will. He had no illusions about the immediate difficulties he was up against. Carisburgh Hall was not a restful place at the best of times and at night the level of din dropped only slightly. There was always someone about. Nurses on night duty bustled around; sheets were changed, nightmares soothed, hot chocolate brewed, dishes washed. It wouldn't be easy to avoid being caught but he had to make the attempt.

"You *could* spend the night there, I suppose," came Miss Brunt's voice from somewhere over his head, "but you'd get pretty uncomfortable."

Martin started and looked around. Ropey Dunning had been sluiced and toweled and led off to bed. The bathroom was quiet and empty. Suddenly Martin discovered how cold his water had grown. Miss Brunt raised an eyebrow and began to mop the floor. Ropey's cleansing had left its mark.

"Have you even started to wash yourself?" asked Miss Brunt.

Martin passed a sliver of soap quickly over his shoulders. It smelt of verbena. Shivering, he lay back to let the suds wash off, his thin body pimpling with gooseflesh. Then he rinsed his seashell and climbed out of the bath. Miss Brunt wrapped him in a towel, toga-style.

"I expect you're clean," she said. "You certainly smell very nice."

Clad in flannel pajamas and camel-colored slippers Martin shuffled back to his bedroom trailing the scent of lemon groves. He quickly got into bed and pushed the covers up to his chin. A young Irish nurse was sitting on Ropey's bed patiently trying to thread the cord back into the waistband of his pajama bottoms. With a squeak of triumph she poked it through on the end of a safety pin, but just then Ropey seized the trousers and with a flourish ripped the cord out again, as if he were trying to start an outboard motor. The nurse passed a hand over her forehead.

"Dear me, Ropey, what a half-witted thing to do! Sure, and I don't care if you sleep with your bottoms around your ankles, 'cause that's where they'll end up."

Ropey climbed into the pajama bottoms but such was his girth that they stuck fast around his middle and stayed up without the cord. He giggled delightedly and bounced into bed. The nurse pocketed the cord and tucked him in. Then she turned out the light, said good-night, and vanished.

Although Martin had intended to remain awake he must have fallen asleep, because the first thing he knew was that Ropey had cried out. Martin lay there quietly trying to gather his wits. Above the door were three glass panels and through these came light from a dusty globe hanging from the corrridor ceiling outside. He waited for a nurse to come but the minutes dragged on and gradually Ropey's breathing deepened into a slow, regular sighing interspersed with gusts. He sounded like someone distantly heard sawing logs in a pine forest on a windy day.

Martin knew it must be late, probably after midnight, because everything was comparatively quiet. There was only the far rattle of dishes and a murmur of voices. Once, a pair of heels clicked their way down the tiled floor outside, past the room and on into the distance. Finally they stopped, a door closed, and there was silence. He waited for another five minutes to make sure, then he eased himself out of bed, put on his slippers and bathrobe and quietly opened the door. The corridor was clear both ways. In his pocket his hand clenched hard over his seashell as he closed the door behind him and glided away down the dimly lit passage. The brown, polished tile gleamed richly; it was like walking along a huge bar of toffee. The rubber soles of his slippers made a sticky sound.

Almost without knowing it, Martin found himself at the head of the main staircase. He had no plan of action, but having got so far, he could see no reason to delay. The main stairs were much used, of course, but at least they were carpeted. Silently Martin flitted past the stained-glass window, which was now black and veined with lead, down into the hall with its armchairs and stacks of magazines. At the bottom he turned left and glided past the silent dining room where the passage lay in darkness, an area into which the hall light could not penetrate. Martin did not know exactly where the kitchen was but he crept cautiously on, following the smell of cold grease that drifted out of the darkness ahead to welcome him. He trailed his hand along one wall as a guide; the smooth stretches were plaster, the corrugated bits were radiators, and the occasional bounce was a pipe. The cooking smell grew stronger. Eventually his fingers found a door without a handle. He leaned warily against it and it opened easily. A whole family of smells slept inside: frying smells and boiling smells, soupy smells and the smell of slops; Martin's entry woke them up and they all crowded around him as he leaned back on the door. It swung shut.

Moonlight seeped through two large windows into the kitchen and splashed dully off aluminum saucepans standing in rows. Along one wall smoldered a vast kitchen range, red gleaming through chinks at the bottom, draft sighing in its flues. Martin moved noiselessly about, carefully avoiding the pots and pans full of potential clatter; but after a complete circuit of the flagstoned room he was as empty-handed as when he started. There was no food here. He looked about and spotted the shadow of another doorway. Once through this he found himself in a pantry, which smelled of stewed tea. On the table in the middle stood a large kettle still warm to his fingers and a huddle of mugs that exhaled the dark sludgy smell of cocoa. There was also half a sliced loaf of bread sprawling out of its burst wax-paper wrapper, several pounds of margarine on a plate with a knife stuck in the top, and an open jar of black-currant jam. Martin set to work turning out jam sandwiches. When he had made six he found a box of tissues standing on the drainboard and wrapped the sandwiches in a handful of them. Also on the drainboard were several apples; Martin helped himself to two. Then he rammed the food into his bathrobe pockets, made sure that every-thing was as he had found it, and crept quietly across the kitchen and out into the corridor.

He stood in the darkness, listening. From some-where upstairs came an occasional muffled sound but as far as he could tell he had the ground floor to himself. Going back was easier at first: the light from the distant hallway guided him and he soon arrived at the foot of the stairs. Now came the worst part. Knowing that the longer he hesitated the greater the chance of being caught, Martin ran swiftly up the stairs, his slippers scuffing on the carpet, up past the invisible woman with her lilies and around the bend. He stopped on the last stair to poke his head into the passage. Now all that lay between him and his bed were thirty yards of toffee corridor. Every yard clung to his feet. He was about halfway along when a door opened at the other end and a hand appeared around the edge followed by the slow emergence of a tray with a teapot on it. Without thinking, Martin opened the first door that came to hand and darted through, closing it behind him. Inside was a warm darkness smelling of laundry. Putting out a hand he could feel shelves stacked with aired linen reaching up on either side of the door. Outside in the corridor feet were coming closer, accompanied by the sound of tinkling. As the feet came level with the door there was the noise of a spoon being dropped; a woman's voice muttered "Damn." Her knee joints cracked juicily as she bent to pick it up. Martin could almost see her trying to hold the tray steady with one hand while she stopped and felt around on the floor for the teaspoon with the other. Then with a hiss of nylon uniform she stood up and the footsteps marched off into silence.

Martin let out his held breath, opened the door, found the passage empty, and fled back to bed, his stolen provisions thudding solidly against his thighs as he ran. Inside his own room once more he sat on the edge of his bed and listened to Ropey Dunning unconsciously replenishing his energy for another day's infantile exertions. Then Martin carefully transferred the food to his bedside locker and got into bed. Although his excursion seemed to him to have lasted a lifetime, the bed was still warm. He heaved a sigh of relief. The only thing he regretted was the jam on the inside of his bathrobe pockets; he put his seashell into his mouth and sucked it clean. It tasted very sweet. He fell asleep in the black-currant smell of his own breath.

4

IN THE MORNING Martin said he had a headache. Aspirin and the prospect of lessons failed to clear it, so Miss Brunt said he could stay in bed if he wished. However, his trick for ensuring a free day would have misfired completely if he had been confined to bed, so Martin said he rather thought fresh air was what he needed most. He was packed off outside with strict instructions to come in at once if his headache got no better.

It was a limp morning full of October damp. The sopping grass wrung the dye out of the toes of his shoes until the leather became a pale bluish color. He had a sudden vision of Miss Brunt watching him from the house. He didn't turn around. He could easily visualize what she could see: a lonely figure hunched into a secondhand overcoat, scuffing a dark trail across the wet lawn and vanishing behind some elms. What Miss Brunt wouldn't know was that his pockets were stuffed with jam sandwiches and apples. Once out of sight of the Hall, Martin took Will's note out of his pocket and carefully reread it. It instantly renewed his determination to help his friend. Because so much depended on his not being caught he was cautious about climbing over the iron fence that marked the boundary of the estate. There was no one about, however, and he quickly set off across the fields on the other side of the road.

He walked in the direction of the coast with a sense of growing excitement. Before all else he had to see the sea. The gulls screamed a welcome around his head as he clattered through a field of cabbages, soaking his trousers from the knees downward. In one fist he clasped his seashell, letting it and the gulls and the salt wind guide his feet. His eyes searched for the first glimpse of the sea but still the land ran on ahead, getting wetter and wetter. Soon the fields gave way to wasteland, and clumps of tough reeds filled a flat marsh that quaked and oozed around his feet. Martin increased his pace, for the tension was beginning to tell; his need to be at the end of this fen was almost a physical pain. Behind him he could feel the Hall pushing him away with all its loveless weight; before him, magnetic prospect dragged him ever forward, the sharp cries of the gulls like spurs, until he pushed through some bushes and finally found himself on a low cliff. And there before him was the North Sea.

It was like two lovers meeting. Martin scrambled down the sandbank onto the shingle, and the sea ran eagerly up to his feet, caressing them. He stood there alone at the end of the land, a tiny figure in a gray landscape. As his ears filled with the welcoming growl of surf, his eyes filled with tears. This was what freedom meant: to be the happy slave of this huge openness, to let the wind whine into his ears. Martin stood for some time looking about him in amazement. The emptiness awed him; he had never been in an empty place before. Yet it was an emptiness that was full of life. The gulls slid about under the icy gray sky and the sea charged at the shingle with powerful exuberance. Here there were no suspicions, no betrayals, no rejection, only the constancy of the waves. Here there were no people.

To his left the beach stretched on and on until it and the sky and the sea joined in a blur the color of Persian cats. To his right the beach vanished around a bend about a half mile away. Some trees screened off this piece of the horizon and from behind them rose a tower or two. This, Martin knew, was the town of Carisburgh. He turned and began trudging along the clinking shingle toward it. Some distance away a thin figure stood motionlessly on the shore. Martin experienced a sudden feeling of annoyance toward the intruder. It wasn't until he had gone several hundred yards farther on that he could see the figure clearly enough to realize that it was simply a gaunt post planted in the foreshore. When he came up to it Martin found a black iron limb about ten feet tall, bleeding orange from beneath scabs of rust. Braced on top was a sort of metal basket. Presumably it was a beacon to warn ships away from the coast or to give them bearings for the port of Carisburgh. He went on again. The beach became narrower and narrower. Here and there the low sand cliff had been bitten into by the waves, and bushes hung on the edge with their roots picked bare. Several tree trunks lay on the shingle, rolled clean. Stealthily, the sea was munching away at the land. After a few more minutes' walking Martin rounded the headland and came upon Carisburgh.

The town was small, although he could see the remains of several large buildings. The towers he had noticed earlier were those of churches, but the churches themselves were empty shells. They stood on the very edge of the sandy cliff, blocks of stone sprawling at their feet, proclaiming their slow ingestion. Blank walls with empty windows leaned into the wind. There were still plenty of houses left standing, however; low, tough buildings that faced the waves shoulder to shoulder. Drawn up on the shingle in front of them a dozen or so sailing boats and on wooden frames nets had been spread to dry. Martin clambered up onto the cobbled path that separated the houses from the beach. He was surprised by the amount of activity going on. Cartloads of sand and shingle were being directed to men with shovels who unloaded them into heaps along the seafront. They worked largely in silence; a grim, threatened silence that had something desperate about it. None of them paid him the least attention. He wandered up one of the narrow streets that led away from the sea. A great wagon of firewood was squeezing down it, drawn by a huge Suffolk workhorse, its shoes striking sparks from the cobbles as its hooves slipped and slid. A smell of seaweed and animals and woodsmoke was in the air.

Everywhere were fishwives in stained dresses, baskets on their heads, dried scales like flaking silver stuck to their bare forearms. They shouted greetings at one another, jostling and pushing. Boys ran, kicking dead crabs or dried mussels down the alley. Shutters were being mended on all sides. Martin sidled along, somewhat frightened by the noise and activity, his mission temporarily forgotten. Suddenly, a hand reached out of a doorway and fastened on his sleeve. He found himself being dragged into a low-ceilinged room constructed of enormous wooden beams, some of which were much scarred and curved like ribs. He knew, without thinking, that they were ship's timbers. He turned to face his captor.

She was a little old woman with a wrinkled face. Her hand gripped him like a claw; for all her apparent frailty she was strong and Martin could feel her nails biting through the material of his coat. He tried to unclamp her hand.

"Oh no you don't," she said. "Granny's made a catch." She pulled him over to a small fire that shivered in a great aching hearth and thrust him down onto a three-legged stool. "Where do you

63

come from, boy?" she asked. "You're not from hereabouts, that's sure. Well, come on, come on." Her old voice screamed at him.

"I am," said Martin. "I'm from the Hall."

"What hall?" snapped the woman.

"Why, Carisburgh Hall, of course."

"Liar!" she yelled. "Stinking cod's head of a liar! The Hall came down in the Great Storm these thirty years ago. Every Christian man in Carisburgh knows that. You're a foreigner, that's what you are. I'll teach you to lie to Granny Mundy. I can tell by your clothes and your voice, boy. You're foreign; you're not from these parts. I watched you coming up the street, don't think that I didn't, and you were lost as a headless eel. Well? Speak up." She shook him. "And the truth, mind. Or I'll curse you into a breadbasket."

Quite what this meant Martin had no idea, but the old woman's tone of voice was enough to convey a certain obscure horror.

"I . . . I'm from London," he stammered.

"Ha!" she shrieked. "Are you? Are you? I *knew* you were foreign." She jerked his arm.

By now Martin was growing weary of the yelling and pulling.

"I wish you'd let go of my arm," he said reasonably. "It's quite unnecessary to keep pinching it like that. I've a perfect right to be in Carisburgh if I wish. As a matter of fact, I'm looking for someone." The thought had just come to him that, old and contentious though she might be, the woman would certainly know where the Seneschal's House was. Now she peered at him with gummy eyes and her grip relaxed.

"Looking for someone, are you?" she mused. "And who would that be?"

"Oh, an old friend of mine," said Martin airily. "Will Howlett. As far as I can remember he lives in the Seneschal's House with his uncle. At least, he always used to."

There was silence while the old woman looked long and hard at him. Then she raised her voice and called "Mary!" Almost immediately, a girl joined them, simply appearing out of the gloom. She was about sixteen with fair hair and very raw hands as if she spent much time gutting fish in the open air. She dropped a little curtsy and looked curiously at Martin.

"Shut the door, girl," snapped the old woman. "Don't stand there staring like a cod." The girl closed the door, and the background noise of the street lessened considerably, although by the warped figures visible through the flawed glass of the window Martin could see that the lane outside was still busy. Covertly, he watched Mary; she reminded him of someone whose name he couldn't quite remember—someone he had once liked.

"Now," said the old woman, and to Martin's surprise her voice had quite changed. It was no longer crotchety and querulous; the aggressive tone had vanished. She smiled. "Please forgive me," she said. "We have to be very careful, you know. Folks are nosy around these parts, but luckily they're superstitious as well. I chase them off by screaming at them—they think I'm a bit of a witch, you see. It's just enough to make them scary, but not enough to make them want to burn me; I take very good care of *that*," she said with a grimace. "I have to do it for privacy; in a place like Carisburgh nobody misses a thing. You were noticed outside, boy; you know that, don't you?"

Baffled, Martin perched on his stool in front of the grate. Unbidden, the girl, Mary, vanished and returned almost immediately with a log of wood under one arm and an earthenware jug of frothy liquid.

"That's good ale," she said, handing it to him and dropping another curtsy. Martin took it hesitantly and sniffed the brew.

"You drink it up," said the old lady. "It'll do you good and you deserve it. You'll be safe here until the boat leaves."

Completely mystified, Martin could only nod dumbly, the tip of his nose white with froth. It was the first beer he had ever drunk and he rather liked it.

"You nearly took me in," admitted the old woman, rocking by the fire in a tall-backed chair. "But we get precious few foreigners here except for *them*, you know, when they come over. You've been told what to do, I expect?"

Martin shook his head. "Nobody's told me anything," he confessed truthfully.

"That's bad," said the woman, frowning. "Perhaps it's as well, though. God willing, the weather will hold until you're safely in France."

"France," echoed Martin flatly.

"That's right," nodded the woman. "The boat will be here tonight. None too soon, either. They've not put in port for over a month and I'm getting low in silks."

"Silks?" repeated Martin. The old woman frowned again.

"They certainly didn't tell you anything," she said. "You'd better know what to expect. I have a shipment of goods coming over from France tonight. Silks, mostly. They'll unload at the beacon and you'll go back with them. There should be no danger; there are one or two spies around but Granny Mundy's fooled them. They're frightened of me. They think I'm a witch." She puckered her face and cackled in imitation of her former diguise. Mary smiled.

Meanwhile, the beer was taking effect on Martin; he was already feeling warm and relaxed. The conversation had been a bit over his head, admittedly, but obviously the old woman had mistaken him for someone else. Equally obviously, though, he ought not to disillusion her. If she had just admitted to being a party to a smuggling organization, she would probably not be pleased to learn that she had given the secret away to a complete outsider. Confident in his ability to avoid trouble in that direction, Martin decided to return to the subject of Will.

"I still want to find Will Howlett," he said. "I'd like to see him before . . . er . . . before I go."

"Ah," said the old woman, "I wanted to ask you about that. I'm afraid I have bad news, boy. Were you very good friends?"

"Yes," said Martin. "Yes, we were. Very good friends."

The old lady leaned forward and put a hand sympathetically on his knee.

"Will was drowned about a year ago," she said. "A terrible business. You know he lived with his uncle Jeremiah? Well, one day Jeremiah took the lad fishing and according to him a wave washed the boy away. Searched for hours, did Jeremiah, but it was dusk and he had no lantern. Since then he's shut himself up in the Seneschal's House and he's gone quite mad. With all respect, he was a mite strange before that, but Will's going has quite addled his brains completely. The devil's taken over Jeremiah Howlett."

"It's true," said Mary, her face white. "The night I took a pail of cockles to Hoggers', why, I run all the way back, I was that scared. Such a noise in the Seneschal's as you wouldn't believe. Ghostly moanings and wailings and wild singings. It was him, all right, fighting with devils. It's a priest's work."

"Aye," nodded the old woman, "yon's no sickness for doctors. Heaven help the poor man. It's all that learning."

"Learning?" asked Martin.

"Love you, yes," she said. "Books—I've never

seen so many of them. Always reading and experimenting with them. Terrible boilings and spells; it's the Black Art right enough."

"Will's dead, then?" asked Martin, hardly believing. Mary and the old woman shook their heads.

"It's certain he must be," said Granny Mundy. "I'm sorry for you. The sea takes many here at Carisburgh," she added bitterly. "And not just our people but our homes as well. You saw the men on the shore?"

"Yes. I wondered what they were doing."

"They're building up a breakwater for the big storm. There's a blow coming. Deaf Peter says there is and he's never wrong, so the men are preparing for it. Not that it will do any good. It made no difference the last time, nor the time before that. We always lose houses. I well remember the biggest blow of all." The creak of her rocking chair stopped; she sat still, as if stunned by the memory. "The year of Our Lord, Fifteen hundred and seventy, it was. Thirty years ago to this very month. Do you know how many buildings were destroyed in that one? Four hundred. Four *hundred*. Houses, churches, palaces, everything. The sea ate them all. This used to be a city with a bishop and even a king, as I've heard tell. Now look at it."

Martin stared out through the bulging panes at the distorted, underwater effect outside. Hooves clopped, dogs barked, wooden wheels ground.

"If you've not been in Carisburgh for a year

or two you'd hardly know the place," said the old woman. "I don't remember when you said you were here last but I expect you remember it when Seneschal's was right next to the Church of All Souls?"

"Oh, yes," lied Martin.

"All gone," said the old woman briefly. "Last year, that was. The storm burst the church doors down. The waves broke over the pulpit. There's nothing left now but the churchyard and still the sea's not satisfied. It's robbing the graves; there are skulls rolling in the surf."

Mary gave a little shriek and covered her ears superstitiously with her hands.

"So the Seneschal's House is pretty near the sea now?" hazarded Martin.

"Right on the edge," confirmed the old woman. "Next time it blows it'll be over, mark my words. But you don't have to worry, do you? You'll soon be in France."

Martin realized with a shock that he had forgotten about his pretended role, so intent had he been on the old woman's story.

"You'd better get some sleep," she advised. "There's man's work to be done tonight, isn't there, Mary?"

The fair girl nodded and winked at Martin.

"Have you got the letters?" she asked him.

"What letters?" Martin asked foolishly. There was a silence.

"Why, the letters from Sir Leonard, boy," the

old woman said finally, a sharpness in her tone. "You've got to have those, of course."

Martin turned a deep red.

"He didn't give me any letters," he stammered. The room grew tense. The two women looked at him with great suspicion. Then a great banging on the door interrupted the silence.

"Wood-oh!" shouted a voice outside. "Only fire'll drive out damp."

At a nod from the old woman Mary opened the door. A stout man in leather leggings stood by a cartload of logs.

"Hello, my lovely," said the gentleman, leering at her. "Would you like something to keep you warm?" Then he caught sight of the old woman sitting at the back of the room. "Begging your pardon, Missus Mundy," he said hastily. "I've brought you some wood for your fires. Bone dry, it is, and will burn hotter than coals."

Instantly, the old lady became a witch again.

"Be off with you," she screamed, "whale-spawn! Or I'll curse that nag of yours into warts."

The woodman paled and put a protective hand to the vast flank of his unoffending Shire horse.

"We must have wood, Mother," said Mary. "Otherwise we'll starve, for we've nothing to cook over."

The old woman crouched in her corner while the woodman started unloading chopped branches. Seeing his opportunity, Martin sprang up and made a dash for the door.

"Stop him!" shrieked Granny Mundy. "Thief! Murderer! Vagabond!"

Mary had turned away and was watching the muscles rippling on the woodman's back with a faraway look in her eye. At this outburst she swung sharply around again but was a second too late. Her grab missed Martin by a hairbreadth as he slipped through the open door and pounded down the cobbled street. Behind him, Granny Mundy's invective died away.

Martin ran until a bright needle of pain in his side indicated a stitch and he was forced to walk. He found himself on the edge of the town away from the sea, where the solid houses gave way to hovels and sties. There was an open rubbish pit surrounded by mud into which were trodden the eyes, heads, and spines of countless fish. Behind the town stretched the bleak Suffolk saltings, the wind gusting sadly through samphire and pines, the marsh birds' calls drifting forlornly in the gray air like wisps of smoke. Martin turned back to face the town. He was worried: the sight of a strangely dressed foreign boy pelting through the streets had not gone unnoticed. Several people had shouted after him and he would surely be grabbed if he ventured back. He decided to make his way around the fringe of the town back to the sea. Somewhere on the sea front, he knew, was the house he was looking for. The old woman had said that the Seneschal's House now stood on the very edge of the sea, so at least it would be conspicuous. He hoped it wouldn't be right in the center of the seafront. But that eventuality wasn't likely. As far as he could remember most of the ruins had been on the outskirts, the central core of houses being intact and obviously lived in by the fishermen.

He found an overgrown path that led around the town toward the coast and pushed his way along it. Occasionally it skirted the ruins of an immense flint wall—presumably dating from the days of Carisburgh's glory—from whose chinks and crannies the dry sticks of dead plants whistled stiffly in the wind. It didn't take him long to reach the sea. Soon he came in the area where the greater ruins stood, empty doorways giving on to the North Sea. Majestic stone portals through which kings and bishops had strolled gave access now only to the wind and the rain and shelter to nothing. A few hundred yards away the inhabited part of the town began, and between it and the ruins, with the waves breaking practically over its doorstep, stood the strangest house Martin had ever seen.

It was quite large, much more in proportion with the nearby ruins than with the small cottages of the town, but to judge by its architecture it was incomplete. At its front was a structure that looked something like a sagging porch crumbling over the low sandbank into the sea. It seemed to Martin that this must be the remains of what had once been a covered way leading to another building, a building now lying beneath the waves. The house itself was obviously ancient and had been pitted and eroded by the continuous assault of the weather. Over the years it had been much patched and mended; there were some antique stretches of flint interspersed with newer areas of narrow Suffolk bricks and in some places even nailed wooden boards covering holes in the structure. There were dozens of windows in different styles: some pointed, some square, some blanked off, and some gaping. Similarly, there were several roofs covering the various parts of the building: some were flat and invisible behind parapets, others were steep and warped. At one corner rose a curious tower that was capped by what looked like a tiled ice-cream cone. Finally, the whole building was covered by vines. Except for a few hardy weeds the weather-beaten façade was bare, kept so by the wind, but the back of the house huddled for warmth in an overcoat of ivy and springs of this and that grew everywhere.

Martin knew that this was the house he was looking for. Even the name Seneschal suited its exposed site; the word had in it the hiss of surf and the bleak rattle of pebbles. Slowly he walked toward the house over the rotting foundations of mints and palaces, and as he did so much of his eagerness left him. The house was frightening. It sat like a dying madman, disheveled and with one foot in a watery grave, glaring at Martin from under bushy eyebrows. It dared him to say it was done for, and as if to assert there was still life in its crumbling body, its breath whistled between broken teeth and its fathomless eyes burned blackly into him as he came hesitantly forward. Trembling, Martin sat down on a fallen arch, its foot resting in the waves. Could there be a living soul inside that house? Was Jeremiah Howlett there? If his nephew Will had been drowned, had Martin therefore received the balloon and its year-old message from a dead person? He looked at the house. Now that he had momentarily halted, some of the defiance had faded from its stare, to be replaced by the extreme tiredness of old age. Pity welled in Martin as he thought of the house's losing battle against time and its proud refusal to die. Will must be dead, he thought. Despair came over him. His friend had called for help but Martin had come a year too late; they were both condemned to their separate lonelinesses.

Miserably, Martin felt in his pocket for his seashell and squeezed it for comfort. His hand also met something squashy and with surprise he took out his black-currant sandwiches. The jam had seeped through the bread and had been blotted by the tissue wrapping but he ate them gratefully; he hadn't realized he was so hungry. He had no idea of the time but supposed it was well into the afternoon by now. He wondered idly what was happening back at the Hall. He must have been missed for several hours and pre-sumably search parties were out looking for him. He munched one of his apples and gazed out over the sea. Three fishing boats were plowing back to Carisburgh, their sails swollen and spray breaking at their bows. Suddenly Martin became aware that the wind had changed. Instead of drifting obliquely across the coast it had veered around more to the north and was definitely stronger. The sea was beginning to look different, too. Instead of the leaden waste there was now movement, and as the waves became more noticeable so the color changed, the hollows becoming darker and the crests lighter. There were also fewer gulls in the air, although one or two followed the little boats into the harbor in expectation of a meal. As he observed the new dimension of the sea, Martin remembered the prediction Granny Mundy had attributed to deaf Peter. There was a big storm on the way, and something in the measured tread of the words the old woman had spoken produced a tingle of anticipation down his spine.

He got to his feet and turned to face the Seneschal's House again. Instantly, the eyes came to life, defying him, but he had made up his mind to go there and make quite sure about Will. He had to be certain: he was too threatened by his own sense of loss to risk letting the matter remain undecided. He gripped his shell hard and walked the rest of the way up to the house. With each step the eyes watched him more and more narrowly. Finally he stood before a great wooden door bleached silver by the salt wind and studded with weeping iron nails. Half the door was covered by an overgrown bush from which a startled bird suddenly exploded, leaving Martin limp with shock. The bird blew away before the wind as Martin searched for something to knock with. There were plenty of loose stones and bricks lying around and from these he selected a conveniently sized piece of coping that had fallen from the roof. Raising it, he knocked timidly on the great door. This produced only a slight thudding sound, so he tried again and harder. The result was spectacular. Martin could hear the echoes dying away inside as if in a labyrinth of halls and passages. The gaunt hollowness of the sound sent a chill through him but then another sound from inside froze him completely. Someone was laughing, deep inside the halls, wild, shouting laughter that chased the echoes of his knocking down dark passageways and throttled them into silence. In counterpoint to the laughs came the slow tread of heavy boots.

Closer and closer came the feet until Martin heard them stop on the other side of the door. He wanted to run but his feet were immovable. He could only stand in mute horror. Slowly the latch rattled and the door yawned. It opened perhaps three feet and then stopped. There was a short pause in which the echoes spent themselves among the stone pillars and arches, which he could dimly see inside. Then a muffled voice spoke.

"State your business and pray for deliverance."

Martin swallowed.

"Are you Mr. Jeremiah Howlett?" he nervously asked the voice.

"Except when the winter moon draws the fog from the fens, I am he."

Martin half glanced over one shoulder to make sure that the moon had not yet risen, but in any case the strengthening wind would soon have dispersed any fog.

"I've come to see you. Or rather," Martin corrected himself hurriedly, "I've come to see your nephew, Will."

"You are a foreigner," said the voice, "or you would know the hideousness of what you are asking." There was a clumping and from behind the door stepped the bizarre figure. Mr. Howlett was tall, his stately physique accentuated by the long black smock he wore. The effect was heightened by the heavy pair of sea boots that encased his feet. Raising his eyes, Martin at first thought with shock that the man had only half a face, for all he could see were Mr. Howlett's deep eyes underneath a mane of tousled hair. Then he realized that the lower part of the man's face was hidden behind a black mask of some material tied behind his head. "Will's dead," said the voice flatly and Martin could see his lips moving underneath the mask, "and all the world knows I mourn him. You have come to torment me; for that you will be punished."

"No," said Martin, terrified by this huge man with the glaring eyes and muffled voice, "you can't do that. I didn't mean to torment you; why should I? You said I was a foreigner, so how could I possibly have known about Will? I'm terribly sorry. I'll go away."

In desperation he turned to go, but the man reached swiftly out in a swirl of black garments and dragged him back by his coat collar.

"Who are you, boy," he growled, "you who have a whelp's nerve to pay a call on Jeremiah Howlett?" He peered closely at Martin. "A foreigner, all right; you're never from Carisburgh. Your clothes are mad." A great laugh roared up from the man's chest and out into the stone corridors inside the house.

Martin recoiled instinctively but the hand still gripped him. When the fit of laughter was over, the man spoke more normally.

"How did you know my Will?" he asked. "How did you know him before the sea took him away?"

This was the one question Martin had been dreading. He had no idea how to answer it, since before Will's death the boy had presumably been living with his uncle and therefore all his friends would have been known to Howlett himself.

"Oh, we met a long time ago," Martin said vaguely and to his great surprise and relief this explanation seemed to satisfy the man, for he nodded his unkempt hair once or twice.

"A long time ago," repeated the muffled voice. There was another pause before he spoke again. "Well, don't just stand there, damn your eyes," he said testily. He had apparently forgotten he was still holding Martin's collar bunched in one fist. A look of cunning came into the fierce eyes. "Come in," he said.

Behind him, the house was a huge crumbling tomb. It was so dark inside that from the doorway Martin could see only those pieces of stonework nearest the light; presumably they stretched away into the gloom beyond. The dank air this gulf exhaled was like a cold hand laid across his face. He backed away as far as he could.

"No, thank you," he said. "I must be going now. I only wanted to see Will. I'm very sorry to hear about him and please will you let me go?"

For some reason, however, the man appeared suddenly to have forgotten about Martin. He was standing there in a kind of trance and his grip had obviously relaxed, for as Martin took another step backward his coat came free and Jeremiah Howlett was left standing in the doorway with one arm still held stiffly out. From behind the mask filtered slurred words, as if he were talking in his sleep.

"The waves march on," he said, "and soon they will do battle. The wind is up—do you hear it? It claps spurs to the sea's flanks."

Martin, speechless, was still backing away from this sinister man. Then the arm dropped and Jeremiah Howlett shook himself. Raising his hands to his head he took great fistfuls of his black mane and screamed into the wind, "Vitriol! Vitriol, you urchin! Vitriol, by the rotting timbers of hell!" Abruptly, he turned around, his black smock billowing and his boots grating on the flagstones, and slammed the door behind him. From outside Martin could hear the dull booming and crashing of boot heels dying away in the decaying house.

Shaken, he turned away. Even during the short time he had been talking the wind had risen still further. It whined around the tattered brickwork of the Seneschal's House like a whipped dog left out in the cold. Inside his secondhand overcoat Martin shivered, unable to decide what to do. Instinct told him to get away from this house as quickly as possible, and now that Will's death had been confirmed there was nothing to keep him here. Close at hand Carisburgh lay under the scudding clouds and the first lamps were being lit behind cottage windows. He noticed also that the fishing boats had been drawn up as far as possible on the shingle and some were even tied to the fronts of the houses themselves, their painters threaded through the iron rings set in the walls. The town was closing up for the coming night and Martin was definitely shut out of it. He didn't belong there; he was an outsider, a foreigner. He could hardly go back; at the very least he would be chased again like a mongrel.

A great loneliness came upon Martin. He stood amid the ruins, a thin, dark boy with the wind wrapping his coattails around his legs. He couldn't stay here, but the idea of going back to the Hall seemed intolerable. Nevertheless, he realized this was what he must do because he had no alternative. Slowly he walked around behind the Seneschal's House, planning to skirt the town and somehow find his way back across the fields. A sudden gust of spray made him turn the corner in order to put the great bulk of the house between himself and the sea and as he did so he looked timidly up at the frowning windows and black roofs. The single round tower at one corner seemed to heel across the sky, but it was only the clouds that moved. Martin was just about to turn his back on the house and walk out of its shelter when a balloon detached itself from the roof at the base of the tower and was swept away in the dusk over the town.

5

MARTIN STOOD IN AMAZEMENT, the wind gusting past the edges of the Seneschal's House, and followed the balloon with his eyes until it disappeared. It had been so unexpected that it took him a moment or two to readjust his ideas. Slowly he understood: unless mad Jeremiah Howlett were sending the balloons himself, Will was still alive somewhere inside that ramshackle prison. The new hope this gave Martin made his mind quicker. Clearly, he had to evolve some sort of plan to rescue Will. After his recent experience he could hardly march up to the front door again and demand his release. But the question that nagged him most was, why should Jeremiah have lied? This was obviously a deliberate plot to deceive the townsfolk of Carisburgh. They all thought Will had been drowned. Jeremiah, evidently, had devised this scheme so that he might keep his nephew imprisoned without arousing suspicion. But why?

One thing was certain: for the time being Martin could do nothing. He would have to wait until he could think of a plan and then come back. A freezing gust of wind prodded him into motion. Sadly he made his way back to the path along which he had come, occasionally looking over his shoulder at the darkening house for any further sign of life. To all appearances, it was as dead as the ruins that surrounded it. There it stood, perched on the shore, its windows opaque, the rising waves just beginning to break onto the porch at the front. For a moment Martin imagined he heard a faint echo from within the house, a distant peal of wild laughter, but it was undoubtedly the wind picking at the bones of the building he heard, compounded by the surf behind him. Helplessly he set off along the path, his thoughts confused. Part of what he felt was happiness. Now he knew he was no longer alone; Will was still alive and his very life depended on him. The other part was a yearning to free Will from that terrible house. Martin's desire for Will's freedom was an ache he couldn't have explained. It wasn't only that he wanted to protect and befriend the boy; in some way Will's confinement actually threatened Martin's own freedom and that was something too new and delicate to risk injuring. The love he felt for the imprisoned stranger, who could do nothing but periodically commend his desire for liberty to the winds, turned into deep hatred of the man who had imprisoned him. All the resentment Martin had ever felt toward those people who had ensured his own detention was now redirected at the wild head of Jeremiah. Apparently on a whim, this madman in mask and sea boots kept his nephew caged like an animal, a sick pet hidden away and desperately calling for help.

Black images flew through Martin's brain as he strode on. It was getting quite dark and he had only just reached the rubbish pit at the rear of the town when he saw a figure coming toward him. It was a woman bent into the wind carrying a dead piglet by the heels. Her skirt flapped wildly and as she and Martin came abreast she stopped. Martin, not wanting to fall afoul of any more of Carisburgh's inhabitants, went on.

"Time to put up the shutters," she called back. Martin halted and looked around. "You'd best be getting home, lad. I don't need deaf Peter to tell me the weather; it's going to be bad. I know it in my bones. God go with us all." She half lifted the piglet in salutation, her other hand clutching her hair. Somewhere behind her a donkey brayed. Silently, Martin waved a farewell and turned back to the path. He didn't know the exact direction of the Hall but he had a rough idea of its location. Although he was returning by a different way, he knew it would be more or less the same distance. At any rate, it was only about a mile away and the countryside was flat. He followed the path past a black huddle of pines that swayed like masts, the wind in their sharp rigging, but after a few more yards the path curved away to his left and he was forced to set off across the wasteland.

By now there was scant light left. Although it was probably not much more than late afternoon, the dark clouds blotted out what little light there was. Behind him over the sea the sky was a uniform purple color and only by the paler streaks overhead could Martin determine that the clouds were racing in tatters above the desolate landscape. It was with considerable relief that he rounded a wood and saw the distant lights of the Hall. A further ten minutes' plowing through sodden fields brought him to the main gates of Carisburgh Hall. As he walked up the drive with the first drops of rain spattering the gravel he began to feel nervous about his reception. After all, he had been out the entire day. In front of the house stood a police car, its revolving red beacon casting a sinister glow. Slowly he climbed the steps and walked into the bright hall, his shoes shedding clods of mud.

"Martin, *dear*," said Miss Brunt. "You're just in time for tea."

"This really is becoming rather a habit, isn't it?" remarked Dr. Herbert, the light gleaming on his pink scalp. He was sitting on the edge of Martin's bed, while Miss Brunt stood solicitously to one side holding a tray. Martin had been fed and bathed and was now leaning back against the pillows with his eyes shut.

"Why did you do it this time?" went on the doctor. Martin opened his eyes. The room was bright and smug. An electric heater had been placed in the middle of the floor to boost the temperature and its warm mechanical smell filled the room. The curtains had been drawn to hide the night that raged beyond the panes but the scourging cries of the wind could be distantly heard.

"Are you unhappy here?" The bald young man tried a third time.

Martin couldn't answer. His return to the Hall had brought with it a kind of deadness he couldn't overcome. The sight of the policemen standing in the hallway, one of them with a flashlight and the other holding a dog's leash, had brought down clanging barriers in his mind. Instantly, his body had become stiff; he had had to be led upstairs like an arthritic, tears running down his cheeks from beneath closed lids. As always, the people around him had begun to shrink. Now Dr. Herbert was a speck, miles away and quite unreachable. Even Miss Brunt was dwindling. She looked like a blue matchstick in her uniform, and when she suddenly put a mug of cocoa into his hands, it was as if the steaming drink had simply materialized out of nowhere. His mind was centuries away in Carisburgh with the sea and the wind and Will in his prison. Dr. Herbert went on asking questions. Unconsciously, Martin drank his cocoa. When he reached the brown silt at the bottom of the mug Miss Brunt said, "I think a good night's sleep, don't you, Doctor . . . ?" Tactfully, she let her voice trail off inquiringly. It was not wise to make self-evident suggestions to a qualified doctor, but there were ways of hinting.

"Yes, he does seem rather shocked," agreed Dr. Herbert. She may be a damn good nurse, he was thinking, but the silly woman does fuss so. "Two hundred milligrams of Amytal wouldn't come amiss," he added aloud.

Soon they put out the lights and left. Martin was finally alone. Ropey Dunning's bedtime was not for another hour and it was hoped that Martin would be asleep well before then. He lay on his back in the semidarkness and looked up at the circular pattern of holes the grille of the heater threw on the ceiling. In one hand he clasped his seashell and in the other a sticky capsule. He had kept it in his mouth when Miss Brunt had given it to him but after they had gone he had spat it out again. The gelatine casing had half dissolved but the white powder inside was still there. For some reason Martin knew it was very important he shouldn't be drugged tonight but it was some time before he realized exactly why. Instantly, he sat up in bed with a jerk, Granny Mundy's words ringing in his head. "Next time it blows it'll be right over . . ."

The Seneschal's House, of course; that was it. The building was already on the brink of the waves. A bad storm would probably demolish much of the front of the house, a really big one might level it altogether; and Will was locked up inside. What on earth could Martin do about it? Hunched in bed, the boy buried his face in his blanketed knees and thought. It didn't take long. Somehow he would have to escape from the Hall again and try to rescue Will. There was no alternative. If Will's life had been in danger beforehand it was doubly so now. Martin was the only person alive who knew of Will's existence, except for his uncle, of course, and Jeremiah Howlett would be the last person to help him get away. Martin tried hard to think; the leaden feeling induced by being back in the Hall was still there, but it was yielding to the urgency of this new situation.

Obviously, the sooner Martin reached the Seneschal's House the better. On the other hand, it was equally clear that he couldn't possibly leave the Hall for some time, not, at least, until after Ropey had come to bed. That would be at seven and after that the night nurse always looked in at around ten. With luck that might give him three hours' grace until his absence was discovered. Martin had no illusions about the dangers of the enterprise; even if he did succeed in getting away there was no guarantee that he would be able to find his way back to the Seneschal's House by night. He listened to the wind howling outside the window and nudging the sheet of hardboard that blocked off the unused fireplace. He thought of the gulls huddled in nooks of rock and then of the creatures that lived deep in the sea, untroubled by its raging surface. In a curious way he longed to join them—to rescue Will and then live forever with him on the seabed, held securely in the bland timelessness. Martin sighed; he knew he could never compete with the cruelty of those who were always chasing him wherever he fled, trying to drag him mercilessly up to the surface again.

As the storm outside grew worse Martin fidgeted in bed, impatiently waiting for Ropey Dunning to come in. Time had suddenly become enormously important to him and each new squeal of wind around the Hall brought him fresh fears about Will's safety. He could imagine the sea already breaking furiously onto the porch of the Seneschal's House. After what seemed like hours of frustration Martin finally heard footsteps stop outside the door and the handle turn softly. As the light from the corridor fell across his face he kept his eyes ostentatiously closed, but when the door was shut again he warily half opened them and saw Miss Brunt ushering Ropey in on tiptoe. At least Miss Brunt was on tiptoe; Ropey clumped despite her hushing. There was the sound of Ropey's clothes being peeled off him, a whisper, a giggle, and the squeak of bedsprings. Miss Brunt, her medal gleaming dully in the light from the stove, turned to go and Martin hastily closed his eyes again. He felt her stop by his own bed and then heard the muffled sounds of the bedclothes being rearranged. There was a pause and then he could hear the soft sound of her breathing and the creak of her uniform as she bent over and lightly kissed the top of his head. Martin lay as still as death.

After she had gone his body took some moments to relax. He listened to Ropey burrowing about like a puppy trying to find a comfortable position. Eventually there was silence. Martin gave him another five minutes, then whispered tentatively, "Ropey?"

There was no reply. He tried again, a bit louder, but still the fat boy gave no sign of having heard. Stealthily, Martin eased himself out of bed and proceeded to dress as quietly as he could, waiting until the very end before putting on his slippers. When he was ready he couldn't resist padding over to the heater and looking down into the top. A gust of scorching air beat upward into his face; he could feel it lifting his hair and drying his eyeballs. A ring of blue flame sat like a coronet at the bottom, its wavering spikes tipped with gold. He leaned over until his face seemed on fire, soaking up the warmth as if in hope of storing it for later use. His hands shook slightly and from time to time he held them out over the stove with the palms downward while he reviewed what he had to do. First, he must go downstairs to the cloakroom and collect his shoes and overcoat, which had been left to dry. Then he had somehow to get out of the building undetected. Thoroughly toasted, Martin straightened up and turned to go. He glanced at Ropey's huddled form but the boy slept on undisturbed.

His journey to the ground floor was more or less a repeat performance of his previous night's escapade. The only difference being that since it was so much earlier there were many more people about. Consequently, Martin took a back staircase instead of the main one. He emerged in the corridor almost opposite the kitchen door, from behind which came the sounds of clashing pans and raised voices together with the smell of fried bacon. He had an idea that the cloakroom was right at the end of the passage but wished he were more certain. He felt utterly naked lurking there with all his clothes on instead of being tucked up in bed. Too many people were moving around; too many doors were opening and closing. Behind the coming and goings was the distant but ever-present booming of the gale outside and this sound alone set Martin's pulse beating faster.

Footsteps sounding at the top of the stairs he had just come down startled him. Hoping his hunch was right, he was flushed from cover into full view of the long, bare corridor. Behind him the footsteps rattled on the staircase, paused at the half landing, then started down again even louder. Martin arrived at the door he was aiming for, turned the handle, and darted inside.

His first emotion was that of relief. Beyond any doubt this was the cloakroom. Quite apart from the unmistakable smells of shoe polish and steaming mackintoshes, the light that had briefly slipped in from the corridor with him had struck the twin row of pipes across which a coat was spread-eagled. Not hesitating for a moment, Martin grabbed the coat and put it on; it was heavy with damp but warm from the pipes. It was certainly his. He had only to thrust one hand into a pocket to feel the stickiness left by his jam sandwiches. When he withdrew his hand, it was covered in burrs of wool. His eyes were by now adjusting to what little light crept under the door; as he turned to find his shoes he saw the line of men standing silently against the opposite wall.

Martin backed away in fright and came up hard against the drying pipes like a prisoner forced against an electrified fence. The shock of scalding metal on the back of his neck jerked him away, and also jolted him, at the same moment, to the common-sense realization that the men waiting for him were nothing other than children's coats hanging from the row of pegs. Trembling with reaction, he stepped nervously over to them and brushed his hand along them just to reassure himself. Underneath the coats were the wooden pigeonholes in which shoes were stacked. He had no idea where his own pair would be but perhaps as they had been soaked, they had been put out to dry. He found them under the pipes. He squeezed his feet into them as if into cases of hot blotting paper. He had just fumbled their mud-stiffened laces into knots when voices approached from outside.

He knew there was no chance of hiding in here; there were no cupboards that he could see; everything was hung or racked in the open. There was a window. . . . The owners of the voices were certainly heading for the cloakroom as there was nowhere else to go at this end of the corridor. The voices became louder.

"Oh, Kitty, *no!*"

"Oh, Kitty, yes. Then she says, very hoity-toity,

'That custard's for the children, *if* you don't mind, Mrs. Thompson.' Well!"

"Cheek!"

"I mean, it isn't as if most of them'd notice if we put *gravy* on their jellies."

"Poor things."

Evidently the kitchen staff was going off duty. Faced with the inevitability of being caught by the women if he stayed where he was, Martin took the only course open to him. As quietly as he could he eased the window up a foot or two, hoisted himself onto the sill, and rolled through the gap into the howling night outside. Behind him the room burst into light and he quickly flattened himself against the wall beneath the window. Above the buffeting wind he could just hear the voices.

"Look, Joan, some silly idiot's gone and left the window open."

"Want their heads examined, some of the people in this place do. And I don't mean the kids, either," the voice of the unseen speaker added darkly. The window crashed down with a thundering of sash weights and Martin was left alone with the storm.

When he had come back to the Hall that afternoon it had just begun to rain. Since then, it must have been pelting, for the ground where he crouched was sodden. The rain hissed down; the light from the window sparkled off a million drops until it suddenly went out and darkness rushed in and filled the space it had left. Martin turned his coat collar up and stepped out of the lee of the house. Instantly, his hair was glued to his skull. He set off into the blackness in the direction of the boundary fence. He would have preferred walking down the drive and out through the main gates, but he was too afraid of meeting some of the staff who lived out of the Hall on their way home. So he tramped across the fields, leaning into the wind, which seemed to be coming directly from the sea. In time he reached the fence, climbed its slippery iron rungs, and dropped without mishap into the road.

By now he was completely soaked. The front of his coat was so wet that the rain made a slapping noise against it. He glanced behind and glimpsed the lights of the Hall winking in a blurred way through the bare bones of intervening trees. Instead of loneliness, a feeling of exhilaration filled him. Somehow the very extent of his wetness and coldness symbolized his new freedom from the institution he had just left. He had joined the world of the gulls and the shells; he moved among the pillars of rain under the heavy roof of cloud as if in a palace of his own. Like a thin little Lear, Martin stumbled off across the black marshes, tripping and landing awkwardly on his heels with jolts that rattled his teeth.

There was no reason why he should ever have found his way back to Carisburgh, but he did. From some distance through the rain he could see a tiny fire flickering in the darkness and he headed toward it. Above the desolate howl of wind there was a new sound, a deep booming that sent elation through him. Soon the rain beating into his face began to taste salty. The fire grew bigger and bigger until he found himself once more standing on the low sandbank overlooking the North Sea. Directly in front of him was the iron pole he had found that morning, a long streamer of flame blowing from the metal basket of blazing wood on top; but now the pole reared out of the water itself, foam breaking around its base. By the orange light Martin could make out three black figures standing in the sea. They had formed a chain to support one another by joining hands. The man nearest Martin passed logs from a pile just above the waterline to the next man, who in turn passed them to the last, who then climbed a ladder tied to the post and shoved the wood into the fire on top. The men were shouting to one another above the noise of the waves and the gale, but Martin could not make out a word. It was a strange, vivid scene, this flickering island in a black waste of wind and water. The light from the flames danced on the sea, gilded the wet iron of the pole, and picked out the white faces of the men as they fought to stay upright while keeping the fire going.

They were fighting a losing battle. Minute by minute the flames grew shorter, the embers lost their white glow and became redder. The man nearest him suddenly let go of his companion and waded back to shore. He had caught sight of Martin standing there watching and climbed up to him. The folds of his clothing poured water; he seemed to be draped in great sheets of wet leather.

"Go back!" he yelled. "Get back to the town and tell them the beacon's done for. We can't keep it alight for more than a few minutes . . ." The wind whipped his next words away. "Tell them . . . no more oiled wood."

He gripped Martin by the arm to emphasize the urgency.

"We've got another half hour, by my reckoning," he added in something less than his previous shout.

"How?" yelled back Martin.

"Tide's turning," answered the man shortly. He turned away toward where his companions were struggling to keep their balance in the waves and his next words flew back on the wind. "Low tide now . . . God save us all." He grabbed another log from the soaked pile and staggered back into the sea.

Martin gave the men one last look and then set off toward Carisburgh. Walking seemed too slow for such an important message but when he tried to break into a trot the marshy ground tripped him. Once he slid into a hollow half full of water and only with difficulty pulled himself out again, his hands slimy with clay. It seemed a long time before he could see the lights of the town. They streamed and wavered as if underwater but at least they were enough to guide him over the last quarter of a mile. He stumbled past the ruins on the outskirts. Here the rain hissed against aging stones, howled through empty windows, and plastered wet plants against decaying mortar. He continually tripped and fell, his feet catching in loose rocks and tangles of undergrowth. To his left he could just make out the huge bulk of the Seneschal's House and he stopped in amazement.

The sea was already breaking under the front windows and washing on and off the decrepit porch. Even as he watched, a great beam of timber was knocked loose and fell into the waves, taking with it a section of the porch roofing in a shower of tiles. It seemed to Martin as if the house were even closer to the sea than it had been earlier in the day. Perhaps this was simply imagination, but each time the sea retreated for an instant to gather momentum there seemed to be less earth and sand at the foundations of the building. There was no doubt that if the tide were really about to turn the Seneschal's House couldn't last. Martin thought of Will locked up inside with mad Uncle Jeremiah stamping around in his sea boots. How he could be rescued Martin had no idea. He wanted to tackle the problem straight away, while there was still time, but he had a message to deliver first; more lives than Will's were at stake this night. Reluctantly, he made his way past the house toward the lights of Carisburgh.

The town was closed up and locked. The houses leaned against each other for support while the wind tore at their roofs and spray lashed their walls. They were battened down, the doors were sandbagged and the windows shuttered. The lights he had seen from a distance were not lights from the houses. Only here and there a chink of light gleamed; most of the houses were in darkness. The lights came from the seafront itself. There, guided by many guttering lanterns, Martin found dozens of men working furiously with shovels to build up the bank of shingle that had, so far, kept the sea in check. Except for an occasional shout, the men worked in silence and also in a kind of frenzy, for it was their own homes they were trying to protect. Even so, the cobbles were already inches deep in seawater and strands of seaweed were wrapped around the hooves of the streaming horses that stood patiently between the shafts of carts laden with shingle. Martin splashed his way over a man in a glistening cape who held one of the lanterns.

"I've just come from the beacon," he shouted.

"What?" yelled the man.

"The beacon. They say they can't keep it alight. And to tell you the tide's on the turn." He saw the man nod.

"That's Alan Hawkins. The beacon doesn't matter now all the boats are in, but why tell us about the tide? We're all fisher folk here, aren't we? We've got eyes."

Martin nodded, nonplussed. The man turned away abruptly and spoke to someone who was holding the reins of a restive horse. His errand evidently accomplished, Martin headed away from the lamps and activity and turned toward the Seneschal's House. In the half hour since he had left the beacon the sea had definitely become higher. The waves struck the low sand cliffs with dull thuds, water washing over the top and up to his feet. In the distance the light of the beacon had shrunk to a forlorn spark and when he looked again a couple of minutes later it had vanished altogether.

The house was still standing, its black roofs jutting starkly into the ravaged sky, but it seemed to Martin that there was a definite overhang now where the foundations lay completely exposed on the seaward side. The biggest waves were already washing around the sides of the house. The sea itself was a frightening presence made worse by being almost invisible. Vague shapes reared up, seen only because they were edged with white surf. It was impossible to tell whether the next wave was going to be higher or not. The noise added to Martin's feeling of vulnerability; so much power so close at hand but only dimly seen was enough to make anyone insecure. For the first time that evening he felt afraid, and he needed all of his conviction to stop himself from leaving this threatened place. His urge for self-preservation told him that he had imagined the balloon that afternoon, that no one was alive in the dying house. He was all alone with the storm and the ruins, and the sea was coming to reclaim the land on which he stood. While he was trying to decide what to do Martin backed away to place the house between himself and the onslaught of the wind and the waves. The slight respite enabled him to think a bit more rationally. The events of the afternoon were beginning to seem unreal. He had just decided to march straight up to the front door and ask for shelter, thereby putting himself in a position to ascertain once and for all whether Will was there, when faintly from within came the chilling sound of laughter. Immediately, the memories of that wild, booted figure with the mask drove all thoughts of this plan out of his head. If he were going to get into the Seneschal's House, he was going to have to break in surreptitiously. He felt along the wall beneath the ivy and found a small leaded window with diamond panes, several of which were broken. Putting his hand through a hole, Martin discovered that he couldn't quite reach the latch. He tried to force his arm through and was surprised to find that the whole window began bulging inward in a sort of patchwork quilt of lead and glass. By this means he managed to raise the latch and swing the window open. The wind caught it immediately and in a flash had wrenched it off the rotten sash, hinges and all, and sent it bowling angularly away into the darkness. As Martin raised a leg to climb inside a particularly heavy crash of waves charged on the front of the house and swirls of white water came around both corners, meeting together at the back and filling the shoe he stood on.

As he lowered himself to the floor inside, the old feeling of elation returned just strongly enough to counteract his dread of actually being in the Seneschal's House and his fear of the rising sea. Perhaps he knew that he couldn't hope to hold on to the feeling long enough to rely on its buoyant effect; subconsciously he turned it into added conviction that Will was waiting for him somewhere upstairs. It was as if he had decided that his pennyworth of courage would be too easily squandered and had instead bought some hopeful capital with it.

He needed it all. The room he was standing in was completely dark. He felt around the walls until he had located the door, which was held shut by a wooden latch. He lifted the latch as silently as possible and gradually opened the door, its hinges complaining in a hideous duet. Luckily, the howl of the storm outside the broken window effectively drowned most of the noise. Martin slipped through, shut the door behind him, and stood listening in the gloom.

Earlier in the day he had come to think of the Seneschal's House as an elderly dying man. From the outside the crippled hulk, with its staring windows and gloomy air, had been forbidding enough from the inside, though, it was terrifying, because the atmosphere of decay was so intensified. Martin was now standing in the skull of this creature, feeling the cooling bone labyrinths emptying of all that had made it human. Once, the house had been alive, and at the height of its affluence had echoed the everyday arrangements of centuries-dead stewards and servants. It had been lived in and cared for; it had been an ornament to the Great Hall now beneath the sea. In those days it had stood securely in the center of a fortified city surrounded by walled medieval gardens of juniper and honeysuckle. Gradually, like reserve troops brought nearer and nearer to the firing by frontline deaths, the Seneschal's House had unwillingly advanced to the sea as the thinning ranks of mansions went under one by one. Now it stood alone among the ruins, and Martin felt the old house knew that at last its time had come.

From somewhere on the first floor enough light trickled down the stairs and pooled in the hall to enable Martin to get his bearings. Ahead was a short flight of steps leading up into the main entrance hall, which he had earlier glimpsed over the shoulders of the house's bizarre tenant. From what he could see, the architectural hodgepodge of the exterior was reflected in the interior. There appeared to be a riot of stone galleries, timbered fireplace, paneling, and alleys. The air was freezing and wet; it smelled of salt and toadstools. The worst thing of all, however, was that the house was *moving*. Each time the wind gusted or a wave broke against the front the whole house lurched. Wood groaned and window frames stirred uneasily with a scrawny sound. From somewhere came the steady trickle of water and as Martin climbed the three or four steps into the hall he met the first dribbles running across the stones toward him.

He splashed his way to the foot of the stairs and just as he was about to start up he heard the laughter again from close overhead. He froze, and above the noise of the storm his ears caught the sound of heavy footsteps marching back and forth, back and forth, and then stopping. Yet he dared not wait; even as he paused a particularly heavy wave broke outside and a window smashed in the front with a splash and a tinkle. The noise of the sea increased and a draft tore across the hall and up the stairs. Martin sidled up with it, one hand slipping along the slimy banister for support. At the top he found himself on a half landing. The stairs continued up around a corner, which was the way he wanted to go, but first he had to pass the open door of a room from which a shaft of light was coming. He could hear Jeremiah Howlett moving about inside, the nails in the heels of his sea boots grinding and crunching on the stone floor of the chamber. He crept to the doorway and peeped in.

The room was quite large with a high, arched ceiling. Although Martin had often seen laboratories, it took him a moment or two to realize that this place was also set up as a kind of laboratory. It was full of equipment he had never seen in his life. There was a huge open fire, ablaze with logs, with hooks above it from which hung a black iron caldron. In the center of the room stood a table or workbench, which was covered with pans of various sizes, some empty and some full, as were also dozens of glass jars and bottles. Over against one wall was a row of enormous glass bell jars and above these were several bookshelves crammed with leather-bound books, most of them with their spines broken and covers missing. The floor was littered with trampled pages, handwritten pieces of paper, broken glass, and pools of liquid. In one

corner there hung what appeared to be a mummified cat.

In the middle of this medieval scene stood
Jeremiah, every inch the mad alchemist. He was
still wearing his boots, black smock, and face mask.
He was bent over an open book on the table, one
hand holding a guttering candle, his fist white with
congealed wax, and the other holding a dully glow-
ing crucible in a pair of tongs. Suddenly he
straightened his back and looked directly at Martin
with his ferocious black scowl. A great laugh shook
him, raging around the stone chamber and up into
the roof. Then he bent back over the table again.
Weak with shock, Martin realized that Jeremiah
couldn't have seen him because of the light from
the lantern on the table between them. From his
position Jeremiah was surely unable to see anything that lay beyond the lantern. Outside the
house the wind wailed and, glancing downstairs,
Martin glimpsed the glitter of black water. Then,
above the noise of the storm, he heard a rhythmic
thudding, like someone beating on a door. It
seemed to be coming from upstairs. He peeped
around the door of the workroom again, but Jeremiah was, for the moment, engrossed in his book.
Martin nipped across the open doorway and safely
on up the stairs on the other side. The higher he
climbed the louder the pounding noise became and
soon he could also hear a voice shouting, but much
muffled.

After another flight of stairs he arrived outside
a squat wooden door set in a paneled wall. An

inch of candle stuck in a sconce opposite flickered bravely in the draft. On the other side of the door someone was beating with his fists, the dullness of the sound testifying to the thickness of the wood. The door itself seemed to be secured merely by a simple wooden latch, a stouter version of the one downstairs. Again there came the crying from the other side and Martin could at last make out the words.

"Uncle! Please, Uncle Jeremiah, let me out. Please . . ." The door snuggled heavily into its frame as the person on the other side kicked it. There was a muffled cry of pain. "Uncle! *Please* let me out . . . I'll do anything. The house isn't safe . . . Oh, I don't want to die, I don't want to die . . . UNCLE!" The voice rose to a thin scream.

Horrified, Martin eased up the latch and leaned his weight on the door. It swung open and he stepped into the dimly lit room, automatically pushing the door to behind him. He didn't want Jeremiah's suspicion aroused should he come up the stairs.

It was a small, beamed room with a bed and a table on which stood a lantern. Near Martin, but steadily backing away from him, was a wide-eyed boy of about his own age dressed in a ragged jerkin and breeches, his white face half hidden in a tangled shock of blond hair.

"Who . . . who are you?" whispered the boy, still retreating. "How did you get in?"

"My name's Martin," said Martin simply, "and

I got in through a window downstairs. I had to break it," he added apologetically.

"But my uncle?" asked the boy, who was clearly terrified. "What did Uncle Jeremiah say?"

"Your uncle doesn't know I'm here," Martin assured him, "but he soon will unless we're quick. You're Will Howlett, aren't you?" The boy nodded. "I found a message of yours tied to a funny sort of balloon yesterday," went on Martin, "so here I am."

Will sank down on the edge of his bed and put his face in his hands.

"It worked," he said as if talking to himself. "My God, it really worked." He looked up again and Martin saw the glint of tears. "I never believed anyone would come," he said. "Do you know, I've been here a year . . . what did you say your name was?"

"Martin. And I think we ought to get going while the going's good; it wouldn't do to get caught by your uncle. He's downstairs in that workroom place of his."

The other boy sprang up in alarm.

"We must go at once," he said. "Uncle Jeremiah would go wild if he found you here. He doesn't allow anyone to set foot in this house, ever."

"Quite apart from that, it sounds as if the place is steadily coming apart," said Martin, trying to keep his voice from showing how frightened he was. The attic room was windowless but the storm outside had grown so violent that they could easily hear the crash of waves and gurgling of water.

Every time a wave thudded against the foundations the house shuddered and its timbers creaked, the wind whining about the eaves. It was like being in a sailing ship.

"Don't you want to take your coat or anything with you?" asked Martin. "It's awful outside."

Will shook his head.

"I haven't got anything," he said.

"Well, as you know your way around this house better than I do," said Martin, "you'd better lead on."

Will crossed to the door and felt for the edge. Then he turned uncomprehendingly to Martin.

"But it's shut," he said, his voice high with strain. "You didn't shut it, did you?"

Martin felt a dragging sensation inside.

"Oh no, I don't believe it," he whispered. "I *couldn't* have done anything so stupid. I thought I just pushed it to, in case your uncle saw it open. It must have closed in the draft. You're quite sure it's shut?"

"It's shut, all right," said Will. He went back to his bed and sank down on it. "So near and yet so far," he said, and the note of despair was so pitiful that Martin sat down next to him and put his arm around the boy. "Whatever are we going to do?" sobbed Will. "This storm will kill us, I know it. Is the sea around the house yet?"

"Yes," admitted Martin. There didn't seem to be much point in denying it; they could both hear the waves breaking all around. "There's already water covering the hall floor downstairs."

The boy's sobs increased and he leaned closer to Martin for comfort. Martin wasn't feeling much better himself; he was listening to the distant but unmistakable sound of sea boots slowly coming up the stairs toward them.

6

Urgently, Martin shook the crying boy beside him.

"Quiet," he said, "listen." The sobs became sniffs and then, as Will also heard Jeremiah's ascending footsteps, Martin felt him begin to tremble.

"Why's he coming up?" Martin whispered.

"I don't know," said Will. "Oh, I've had enough; I just want to be left alone."

'No, Will, please listen," begged Martin. "Don't give up yet. Perhaps if I stand behind the door he won't see me. Whatever happens, if you have the chance to get away, take it."

The trudging feet were much nearer now, and with them came another sound, which puzzled Martin at first. He thought it was a new outburst of moaning from the tortured rafters of the old house, but then he realized that Uncle Jeremiah was actually singing. The noise drew nearer and finally stopped with a crash of heels outside. The latch grated and the door swung inward, Martin cowering behind it and being squeezed farther into the corner. He could get an idea of what was going on by peering through the crack in the jamb. The bulky figure of Jeremiah Howlett had its back to him and Martin could just get a glimpse of Will sitting dejectedly on the edge of his bed beyond.

"Aye, it's a wild night, young Will," boomed the man's voice. Will said nothing. "But you're safe here with old Jeremiah," the voice added.

"I don't think you're right, Uncle," said Will faintly. "I think the house is going to fall down soon."

"Nonsense. Why should it? It was put up in twelve eighty-one; why should it fall down in sixteen hundred? But enough of that. In three hours or so I shall succeed in my life's work, Will. I have the answer at last." His voice dropped in volume but rose in intensity. "Gold, Will—all the gold you'll ever want. Gold *for you.*"

There was silence.

"*Well?*" roared out Jeremiah suddenly. "Are you dumb? I tell you, the experiment's nearly over, damn your hide. I am the only person in the history of the world to wring gold out of common lead. After years of work, after slaving for you. For *you,* you sea-puppy whom the world believes drowned; I've made you gold. In three hours I shall show it to you, and all you do is sit there like a simpleton. Well, we'll soon hear you change your tune when I come up with fresh, warm gold in my hands. Huh?"

"But I don't want gold, Uncle," said Will in a small voice, "I want to get out of this house before it collapses." As he spoke, the whole building swayed and again there was the sound of crashing glass from down below. Jeremiah swore bitterly, turned around with a screech of hobnails, and slammed the door. Then he clattered away down the stairs.

"Well," said Martin, emerging from behind the door as the man's footsteps grew fainter, "now what are we to do?" He went over and sat down by Will again, slipping an arm protectively around his shoulders once more. "What on earth's all this about?"

Will wiped his face on his sleeve.

"It's mad," he said. "Or, at least, Uncle Jeremiah is. I'm not even sure if I'm still sane."

"Of course you are," said Martin.

"There's certainly no reason for me to be," Will said, sniffing, "not after a year in this place alone with him. It's probably more than a year now, but I've lost track."

"How did he manage to get you here in the first place?" asked Martin.

"It's a long story," said Will. "What happened was that ever since I was small I've lived here because my mother and father were drowned in a flood. Uncle Jeremiah and Aunt Elizabeth took me in and looked after me. Then she died of consumption and Uncle Jeremiah took me over like

. . . like . . . well, as if I were a sort of field he had to farm. He's always been mad about his old books and mixtures and he thought he could turn me into his apprentice. At that time I used to go to school in Carisburgh, but one day he decided that I'd learned enough Latin and things and that I'd spend the time better being taught by him. I must admit, I was interested; he's pretty clever, I suppose. But then he pretended to kill me off."

"Ah," said Martin, "he spread it about that you'd been drowned so your absence would be explained."

"Exactly. That's what he did. One day he wouldn't let me out of the house and he put on black clothes and turned people away if they came to visit us. I've been here ever since."

"But that's awful," protested Martin. "I suppose you tried to escape?"

"Oh, yes," said Will bitterly, "I tried to escape, all right, but after he caught me twice he just shut me up in here and here I stay, a prisoner, except when I'm working with him in that room of his downstairs."

"I know how you feel," said Martin after a pause. "I've been a prisoner, too."

"Were you fed?" inquired Will listlessly.

"Regularly," admitted Martin.

"I'm not," said Will. "Sometimes he forgets for days."

"What's all this about gold?" asked Martin. Will laughed shortly.

"He's mad about it, that's all," said the boy.

114

"He thinks he can make it and so he spends all his time trying."

"And can he?"

"I really don't know," answered Will seriously. "I think we've come pretty close sometimes. He's very clever, there's no doubt about that. I wouldn't be surprised if he had done it. We were working with lead, actually; we certainly discovered some funny things along the way. Like light air."

"What's that?" asked Martin curiously.

"Light air is what made my messages fly," said the boy with a touch of pride. "We discovered it by accident. We were making some oil of vitriol by the bell . . . you mix sulfur and niter in one of those bell jars and burn it."

"I saw the bell jars downstairs," said Martin.

"Well, it's called making vitriol by the bell," said Will. "It's all in Latin, *per campanum,* or something, in one of Uncle Jeremiah's books. Anyway, I spilled some of it on a heap of old nails and saw that it was fizzing and bubbling, so I put it all in a jar to collect the bubbles. We did lots of tests with it and eventually discovered that it was lighter than air, so I called it light air."

"That's amazing," said Martin in admiration. "I wonder if it's like hydrogen?"

Will shook his head.

"I've never heard of hydrogen," he said, "and I've heard of most things in alchemy. No, it's called light air, all right. Then I thought, well, if you can make bubbles float perhaps a lot of light air would make a bladder float. So Uncle Jeremiah got one and we tried it and it worked. Then he said it had nothing to do with making gold so he wouldn't let me go on making light air."

"How did you manage to send the messages, then?"

"Mice," said Will.

"Mice?" queried Martin, baffled.

"Yes, didn't you see them? I couldn't make a balloon light enough until I suddenly thought of all the mice in my room. I set traps and caught dozens. Then I skinned them, took the fur off, and scraped the skins as thin as I could. At the end I sewed them together with fine silk. You have to wax the seams," added Will, in case Martin was thinking of trying this experiment, "otherwise the light air gets out. They take hours to make and I have to be careful because Uncle Jeremiah's terribly suspicious. He's nearly caught me filling the balloons several times, because he hardly ever leaves me alone in the laboratory for more than a minute. I had to release them through the laboratory window too."

"It's incredible," said Martin. "How many of these things have you made?"

"Only four," said Will.

"*Four?*"

"Yes, it stops me from going mad. All this talk about gold the whole time; and he says he's doing it for me, so I can be rich."

As Will talked he became more and more animated and now he was looking quite cheerful.

Martin knew it must be a great relief for him to have someone other than his uncle to talk to. Indeed, they had both become so absorbed by the narrative that they had temporarily forgotten about the storm outside and the wild, raging man brewing gold downstairs. However, the shaking of the house was now becoming too violent to ignore any longer. It was clear that they had little time left.

"There must be a way out of this room," said Martin.

"There isn't," Will said, shaking his head. "I've sat here for hours at a stretch trying to work out how to escape, but it's impossible. I think it's the only room in the house without a window, which is presumably why he keeps me in here, damn him."

Martin understood Will's vehemence only too well. He looked at the shut, handle-less door, the undulating floor, and the arched garret roof supported by the same kind of curved beams he had first seen at Granny Mundy's house.

"Ship's timbers," confirmed Will, who had been watching Martin's inspection; "solid oak." At that moment an enormous fist seemed to grab the house as the floorboards heaved and cracked and the air became full of dust and the scream of wooden joints being torn apart. Martin and Will staggered as the Seneschal's House momentarily lost its footing, then resettled uneasily into a lopsided and obviously temporary position. They could hear tiles cascading down the roof above their heads and some plaster fell away from the wall by the door and slid across the newly canted floor. The whole building seemed so unsafe that it was some moments before Martin and Will dared shift their positions for fear of upsetting the delicate equilibrium. Both were now convinced that they were shortly going to die and both were reacting differently. Of the two, Will was the more philosophical; perhaps resigned would better describe his attitude as he perched gingerly on the edge of his tilted bed. After all, he had given up hope so often in the last year that it was becoming a habit he slipped into quite easily. Martin, on the other hand, had only just tasted freedom and was far less prepared to relinquish it without a struggle.

He glanced around to see if this new upheaval had altered the situation in any material way and noticed that the door appeared to have moved along the wall. There was now a considerable gap between the frame and its plaster surround on one side. He moved across to investigate further when the candle, which had lately become a worm of burnt twine in a decreasing puddle of tallow, winked out. Will's wail of dismay from the bed coincided with Martin's shout of excitement. Through the newly opened gap in the wall he could see the light from the candle outside—the hole went right through.

"Will, come here," he cried jubilantly. "I think there's a way out, after all. Have a look at that," and he steered Will into a position from which he could see the light.

"What are we waiting for?" asked the boy when he had grasped what had happened. "Let's get out quickly; the next time the house moves the hole might close up."

"Well, go on through," said Martin, putting a hand on his shoulder, but Will suddenly pulled back.

"Just a minute," he said, "I've forgotten something. You go on." Will felt his way over to the bed. Martin could hear him fumbling in the darkness but remained standing where he was. "All right," said Will a moment later, "I'm ready now." He slid his thin body into the gap and wriggled through. Sections of dislodged plaster fell with thumps onto the floor. His voice came back to Martin, "I'm through, come on," and Martin followed, the buttons on his overcoat clicking on the stonework. It was a tighter squeeze for him because he was wearing more clothing but Will grabbed one of his hands and pulled. Soon they were standing together outside the room, breathing heavily; then Will led off down the stairs without wasting another moment.

They tiptoed down until they came to the bend around which oozed the glow from Jeremiah Howlett's laboratory. Their stealth was probably unnecessary, for the noise was now frightful. The house groaned, the wind tore and roared, and the sea was flooding in waves through the broken ground-floor windows. Will, in the lead, snatched a glance around the bend in the stairs, signaled caution, and went down. He peered carefully around the door of his uncle's workroom and motioned with his hand for Martin to follow. Martin crept up beside him and together they watched what was going on inside.

Jeremiah was kneeling on the stone floor to one side of the fire into which wet soot dislodged by the storm was falling in a hissing rain. His smock was tucked up around his thighs and his shanks gleamed whitely in the firelight, long thin lengths of apparently dead flesh incongruously joining the sea boots to the great body. He was intently packing a shallow wooden box with a silk handkerchief. When he had finished he scrabbled around on the floor and found a blank sheet of paper half lying in a pool of water. He tore off the dry portion, found a quill pen from somewhere, trimmed the nib with his teeth, and dipped it into a cup of ink on the table. He laboriously wrote a few words on the piece of paper, folded it, and put it in the box. Then he went to a crucible standing on a brick in the hearth, picked it up with a pair of tongs, and dropped it into an earthenware pot. There was a splash and a violent boiling sound; clouds of steam gushed from the mouth of the pot while Jeremiah sat back on his heels and chuckled, his great hands resting on his thighs. When the bubbling had stopped he squinted into the pot and fished about with the tongs, finally coming up with the dripping crucible, which he then turned upside down. A gleaming yellow object fell into his left palm. It must have still been very hot for he immediately transferred it swiftly yet gently to the silk-filled box with his fingertips as though it were a lightly boiled egg.

"Gold," he said in an intense voice of almost religious awe. "Now that *is* a present, my Will." He bedded down the tiny pellet of metal in the handkerchief, laid the note on top, and put the lid on the box. Then he climbed noisily to his feet, the heel of one of his boots striking a line of sparks from the stone floor.

Martin and Will had watched this ceremony with mixed feelings. They could neither of them ignore the distaste with which Jeremiah filled them but it had been modified by a feeling of almost pity. There was something moving about seeing this huge, uncouth man trying to make a little present out of an old box and a handkerchief, and for a moment it had seemed that those dark, threatening eyes above the mask had softened into an expression of tenderness. Then the man turned around and began clumping toward the door. Too late, Martin and Will realized their mistake in not passing the open doorway when they had had the chance; there was now only one way left open to them: back the way they had come. They turned and raced up the stairs, just getting around the corner as Jeremiah emerged from his room.

Will led the way to the door of his former prison. Behind them his uncle's feet pounded on the stairs.

"We can't go back in there," panted Will. "I couldn't stand it. We'll keep on going up."

Just past the door there was another flight of

stairs, a narrow corkscrew that presumably wound its way up the tower Martin had noticed from the outside of the house. They started to climb it but didn't get much beyond the first turn before Jeremiah reached the top of the stairs below. Immobile, they listened to him lift the latch of the door and go into the room. There was a short pause and then an unearthly cry echoed through the house. It was as if a bull, mortally wounded by a matador, had suddenly been able to speak at the moment of truth.

"Will!" he roared, his boots stamping and pawing the floor below. Faint tremors reached the two crouching listeners and wood creaked ominously. "Where are you, boy?" There was more stamping and then a louder crash. It sounded as if Jeremiah had overturned the bed in his anguish, presumably to see if his nephew were hiding underneath. Then Martin and Will were horrified to hear a new note in his voice. The huge man was crying.

"He's gone," sobbed Jeremiah, "the faithless puppy. Gone, like a cheap traveler slipping out of an inn without paying." There was the sound of falling plaster. "Crept through the wall, he did, and left me. Oh, damn him, damn him utterly."

In the darkness Martin put a hand around the shoulders of the boy who stood trembling beside him.

"He doesn't want my present," Jeremiah's voice choked as he banged about the room. "Twenty years' work finished tonight, work done for him, and at the very moment I finish he slips away . . . Oh God! The cruelty of it . . . the *cruelty.*"

There was a noise of splintering wood and then the voice added tiredly, "You may yet be lurking downstairs like a drowning mouse; I'll see. Don't think because I love you like a father I'll tolerate your mischief. I'm coming down, my Will. Will? I've got a present for you . . ." the words faded suddenly as Jeremiah turned the corner of the stairs on his way down to the bottom of the house. Windows banged in the gale; the tower rocked.

Beside him, Martin felt Will crying. Some half-remembered tone in the voice had brought tears to his own eyes, too; some emotion he had once felt had been stirred again by Jeremiah's outcry, the hopelessness of those who can only express their love in unacceptable ways.

"Come on, Will," he said gently at last. "We really must get out; we'll just have to risk meeting him."

Will didn't answer but sniffled as he got up from the step on which he had sunk. They went downstairs and had just reached the laboratory when once more they heard Jeremiah coming up the stairs toward them. Will groaned. Refusing to go back yet again, Martin led him into the dim room and they waited there behind the door for their inevitable discovery.

The footsteps seemed to have slowed considerably. They dragged up the steps, paused on the threshold, and then came into the room. The floor shook. From their dark place of hiding, Martin and Will could see most of the room. They watched as Jeremiah crossed to the great open fireplace, and as the light from the fire and the lantern he was carrying fell on him, he half turned. His clothes were wet through and a pool formed around his sodden boots as he stood there. His smock was torn and his hair was so fantastically tangled into spikes and cowlicks and quiffs that it was like a sculpture in black wire. But what shocked Martin and Will into numbness was his face. Unnoticed, the black mask had slipped down around his neck and for the first time they realized why he wore it. Jeremiah had been terribly disfigured from his cheekbones to his chin. Almost as if he sensed their stares he brought his hand hesitantly up to his face and felt for the protecting material. He blinked and then shook his head roughly.

"Too late," he said to himself, or perhaps he was talking to the mummified cat that swung stiffly a few feet away, "all far too late. I think you've gone, Will, I think you've gone." He passed his hand completely over his face, tracing the edges of the scar. "Molten metal did that, boy," he said to the silent cat. "Never forget, Will, the road to gold is paved with boiling lead." He sighed. "You would never believe me—perhaps you wouldn't even care—but I was once not ugly at all. I am ugly now because of gold—and because of you."

The whole house surged as waves broke

around it. Somewhere overhead a section of roof fell through into an attic with shattering noise. Jeremiah looked up at the ceiling; the dried cat bobbed on its string.

"Perhaps you've risen, Will, with your light air," he remarked musingly. "If you're not downstairs, then maybe you're up. I've still got your present," he added sadly as he took the lantern and trudged out of the room. Martin and Will listened to his boots plodding up the stairs and then roaming about heavily overhead. Stiff with cold and tension they tiptoed out of the laboratory and down the main staircase to the hall. It was an amazing sight. The bottom steps were covered by water that surged over the entire ground floor. The front windows had gone; all that was left were ragged holes in the brickwork through which the North Sea was breaking. The air was full of spray and the noise of water trapped in the stone hall was deafening.

"We'd better go out the way I got in," shouted Martin above the din. "We'll never get out through the front."

They stepped off the stairs into the bitter sea, which came up above their knees. There was quite a current running in the hall; the water sucked and foamed in and out of the corridors and niches, swirling around the foot of the staircase. Broken furniture and window frames bobbed on the tide. Martin helped Will toward the door that led to the back room he had entered through. At the last moment he remembered the short flight of stone steps leading down to it, but it was too late. The current pulled them both over. Instantly, they were off their feet. Paddling desperately, they were swept past the door they were aiming for and then, as a counter-surge met them, swept back again. As they passed, Martin managed to grab the latch of the door under the surface of the water and hold on. He lifted it and pulled at the door. It opened a few inches.

"We've got to get through here," he spluttered, thrashing the water to keep up his head. Together they pulled. Had the water been only on their side of the door it would have been impossible, of course, but the room beyond was filled to the same level and so the pressure was more or less equal. Even so, it took a great deal of effort to pry the door open while the waves threw them about and broke their grip. But at last they were through. In the back room they were able to wade through water that was comparatively calm.

The window through which Martin had climbed looked out over an awful scene. The Seneschal's House was at sea. Outside, the black water rushed and broke in spray against the nearby ruins. Common sense told them that it wasn't more than three feet deep, but it looked thirty. Across the wild expanse a few lights twinkled, so evidently there were houses still standing in the town. At that moment a great rumbling came from the front of the house and a wave surged in from the hall, lifting them and smashing them painfully against the window ledge. Through the open doorway behind they glimpsed a hole in the front wall of the house through which the sea was pouring. The structure overhead moaned and swayed.

"It's coming down!" yelled Will.

"Out of the window, quick!" Martin urged him, helping his friend over the sill and following him. Some dislodged masonry fell into the water nearby. Together they plunged away from the house but it was like trying to run in a nightmare. The water slowed them to an agonizing wade, but gradually, as the ground behind the house rose slightly, the going became easier. At last they reached the raised foundations of a ruined church and turned in only a foot of water in time to see the end of the building they had just left.

The Seneschal's House rose like a mad galleon out of the pitching black waves of the North Sea. Its wry roofs dipped, its chimneys had snapped and fallen through great rents into the main body of the house. Even at a distance of some sixty yards the noise the house made in its death throes was awesome. Great beams broke like twigs as the sea swayed the walls into contorted slabs, gunshots of splitting wood sounding out across the floods. Joists leaped from their ancient beds at this last awakening and ceilings fell inside, huge clouds of gray dust puffing out of the smashed windows to be ripped into shreds by the gale. Martin realized that the house had already died; the once-threatening windows were now blank, the bushy eyebrows of foliage torn out by the roots. The spirit had gone but the body remained to be broken up. Inside, the sea ran around the cage of its bones, splintering them with clubs. The skull cracked across and rafters poked through the wound.

Suddenly Will grabbed Martin's arm and pointed wordlessly. At the top of the tower a light had appeared in a window and a dark figure was framed there. Even from this distance they could see Jeremiah Howlett's mass of wild hair as he stood motionlessly looking out over the ravaged landscape. A massive wave broke against the front of the house, spray shooting up as high as the eaves and for an instant almost hiding the entire building. As it fell, the Seneschal's House fell with it, folding up with an uncanny lack of noise. The lonely figure at the upper window raised a gowned arm as if in salutation to someone he knew was watching and then the roof slammed down. The sea seemed to erupt to receive the house, which slid almost in relief down over the sandbank to collapse with a roar in the surf. When the spray had cleared, there was only a ragged island of rubble to mark where it had stood. A small wave broke over their shins and shocked Martin and Will back to reality.

"Poor Uncle Jeremiah," said Will softly into the wind. Martin couldn't hear the words but he knew what they were. He turned Will gently away from the grave of the house and led him toward the scattered lights of Carisburgh.

From some distance away it was clear that the damage to the town had been great. Although it seemed to Martin that at last the ferocity of the storm was easing, the water still reached well into the center, marooning the first row of houses along the seafront. These had evidently been well built, for with the exception of one or two gaps they jutted up in a stubborn curve like teeth in a jawbone. Martin and Will headed for the higher ground toward the rear of the town, rightly assuming that all the inhabitants would have gathered there. They splashed out to the place where Martin had met the woman with the piglet. There they found the townsfolk huddled together under hastily improvised shelters. Crouched beneath glistening oilskins, they looked like outcrops of some monstrous fungi, their pale legs seemingly growing out of liquid mud. Those that could crowded into houses of people lucky enough to be out of the sea's reach. Those who were left pressed up against walls under streaming eaves while the rain whipped them into submission. Soaked children whimpered as the wind slipped icy fingers through holes in their clothes and picked their carefully hoarded pockets of warmth.

Martin and Will stood among the people and looked down the main street toward the sea. Waves were breaking on the cobbles halfway up and water was eddying out of doors and windows smashed by the storm. Out of the North Sea came three men carrying an old woman. She had evidently been trapped in one of the houses that formed the semicircle on the seafront. Martin could see a light still burning in its distant upstairs bedroom. Even as the men reached safety and turned to face the sea they had saved her from, a window in her empty cottage tore loose and the light inside flickered and vanished as the draft overturned the candle. Then a low cry went up from those watching, for in place of the candle-light an orange flower began to grow, its bright petals swiftly blooming from every window. Smoke and sparks glowed on the wind. The old woman waited in silence until the roof of her house fell in, her seamed face wet with rain. Then she walked through the mud with great dignity to the nearest doorway, the crowds inside standing back to let her in, and disappeared inside. On the sea-front, the waves swamped the embers, and the spectators' eyes were fixed on the spot long after the last flame had died.

The storm had definitely passed its peak. The wind was dropping and even the rain had eased. In the tower of the flooded church the clock, incongruously, struck five and the fishermen looked at one another.

"Tide turns in a minute," said a man with a bushy beard, whose left hand hung across his chest in a makeshift sling.

"Aye," answered the man next to him, "aye. With luck that's the last of it. Until next time," he added.

"Do they know who's missing?" asked the bearded man. His friend shook his head.

"Last I heard there was twenty folk not seen. You know Dave Runnacles is gone? Him and all his family. Five of them, that is."

The man with the beard shook his head mutely.

"Jeremiah Howlett's gone, too," broke in Will suddenly. The men turned to look at the bedraggled boys behind them.

"Is he?" asked one. "Poor mad soul; heaven spare that one." Then the man peered more closely at them. "Well, who the hell are you?" he asked. "You look powerful like his young nephew Will."

"I am," said Will simply. "Hello, Mr. Jevons."

But the men were backing away. The townsfolk around stirred in their apathy like cattle and whispers flew sibilantly behind cupped hands. Then suddenly a woman shrieked hysterically, "It's Will Howlett. Oh my God, he's come back. The sea's brought him back to haunt us."

A wave of fear swept through the crowd and people began pressing away from Will and Martin. When they found they couldn't get far because of those crushed behind, panic changed them into terrified animals. They all turned, screaming, and scattered out over the town, their cries and running footsteps dying away in its lanes and alleys. A priest in a mud-stained cassock was the last to go. He backed away over the wet cobbles, driven by the inner conflict between faith and fear, at a brisk pace that was a nice compromise between standing his ground and outright stampede. Then he, too, vanished. Doors slammed, bolts thudded into sockets, and silence fell. Will and Martin were left standing alone in the street among the cold puddles.

"We must go," said Will at last. Martin could hardly hear him.

"Where to?" he asked.

"Anywhere; I don't know. I'm so tired. I want to be free of this town and these people and the sea."

He turned and splashed slowly toward the pine forest behind them. Martin walked with him in silence. At the edge of the trees they came to a sty huddled in the shelter of a windbreak. Will climbed wearily over the low wall and felt his way inside. Martin found himself in pitch darkness that smelled of hot pig and straw. There was an outburst of disturbed grunting and squealing over in one corner, a confused, but brief, jostling and thrashing. Martin felt Will's hand guide him up to a ledge a few feet off the floor.

"It's where the straw's kept," said Will. "I used to help Mrs. Banty with her pigs; they were always very clean."

They sat there huddled together in the warm darkness and gradually their frozen bodies thawed out, the involuntary shivers grew less violent, their teeth stopped chattering, and their clothes turned from wet to damp.

"I never thanked you," said Will. Martin made a deprecating gesture in the blackness.

"I'm sorry about your uncle," he said. He heard Will sigh.

"Poor Uncle Jeremiah. I still can't believe I'm no longer a prisoner there; it's incredible."

They both fell silent. Then at length Will said, "Do you know, I never realized about Uncle Jeremiah. I mean, about him doing it all because he loved me, and getting burned and things. I just thought he was cruel and mad. He used to hit me if I didn't do what he wanted. If I tried to run away or made a mistake in the laboratory he'd just beat me." Will began sobbing again as he remembered his life during the past year.

"How could you have known," Martin asked him, "if he never gave you a chance to find out? How can you go on hitting someone and then at the end claim you were doing it all for love? It's not fair. Honestly, Will, you mustn't feel guilty."

"I suppose not," gulped Will. "It's just that . . . I don't know, he looked so sad. And lonely, too, wandering about Seneschal's with my present." The tears came afresh.

Beside him, Martin put an arm comfortingly around his waist and let him cry. He felt nothing but a great tenderness for his friend. Gradually, the sobs subsided.

"Incidentally," said Martin, "you remember when you were just about to go through that gap in your bedroom wall and you said you'd forgotten something? What was it?"

"Oh, nothing," said Will. "Just a sort of lucky mascot I've got."

"I've got a mascot, too," admitted Martin encouragingly.

"It's the skull of the first mouse I caught for my balloons," said Will. "It was under my pillow. I suppose it seems silly, but I was really sorry I killed it. It was the only thing I could think of, though."

"I know exactly," said Martin.

"Honestly?" asked Will. "It sounds crazy. I boiled the skull clean and I used to talk to it for hours and hours; there wasn't anybody else, you see. Except Uncle Jeremiah, and he was . . ." His voice tailed off expressively. "Hang on," he added, "I've got it here." Martin could hear him fumbling. "That's odd," said Will in the darkness, "I think I must have lost it."

"Perhaps it got washed out of your pocket while we were swimming about in the house," suggested Martin.

"It's possible. Yes, it's gone, all right. Oh well, I don't need it now, after all. I'm not a prisoner any more and anyway, I've got somebody real to talk to now."

Martin was suddenly aware that he could see his hands. He looked up and the doorway was a frame of gray in the surrounding darkness.

"It's getting light," he said. "It's dawn."

They went outside a little later. The wind had dropped and the wrenched clouds drifted exhaustedly across the sky. Carisburgh was a study in gray, as if the battering it had received during the night had wrung all the color out of it; yet there was somehow a lack of monotony. The sea and sky were of different tones in the dawn shadows that lay across the town.

People were walking about as Martin and Will headed down the main street. Most of them looked numb and dazed, for although nobody in Carisburgh had slept, all had experienced a nightmare. This cold dawn seemed unreal, as did the events of the night, and now people, who only a few hours before had run screaming from Will, peered at him flatly from behind doorways and sodden curtains. Eventually one woman, bolder than the rest, came out. Will smiled.

"Hello, Mrs. Banty," he said.

"Will!" cried the woman. "It really *is* you? God be praised, child. Come in, both of you."

They followed her into her cottage, where her husband was on his knees trying to light a pile of damp kindling in the hearth.

"John," she cried, "look who it is. It's young Will Howlett come back with a friend."

"Well, bless us all," breathed Mr. Banty, rising, the look of alarm on his face changing to one of happy recognition. "So it is. Dang me, boy, where did you come from? There was folks here last night saying they saw you walk out of the sea at the height of the storm on King Neptune's arm."

Will shook his head, laughing.

"It can't have been last night," he said. "Martin and I were far too busy trying to escape from Seneschal's. It's down at last," he added.

"The old Seneschal's House?" asked Mrs. Banty. Will nodded.

"And Uncle Jeremiah with it," he said. While Mrs. Banty tried to heat milk for them on the smoldering fire he told the story of his imprisonment and Martin's last-minute rescue. As he spoke, neighbors peeped fearfully in through doors and windows, pushing closer and closer until by the end of the tale the low room was crammed with people welcoming Will back from the dead. Before long the whole town knew, but the rejoicing was considerably muted by the tragedies of the storm. For every person who was happy to see Will back, there were ten who mourned those they had lost. Nobody stayed long in Mrs. Banty's house, there was too much work to be done. In their turn, Martin and Will joined the people in the streets.

The damage was horrifying. Nearly all the cottages on the seafront were ruins, and where they were still standing at all they were little more than damp shells. The one that had been gutted by fire and water stared blankly out to sea, roofless and blackened. Thirty-one houses had been destroyed, including the Seneschal's House, and many more badly damaged. The cobbled streets were littered. An occasional tile still slid off a roof and plopped into a pool below, joining the bricks that lay everywhere. Seaweed festooned the town like leftover decorations from some marine festival, bundles of it collecting along the seafront and draping the hitching rail by the jetty with what looked like wet chamois. It was as if the sea had given Carisburgh a foretaste of what history had in store for it.

Among the tons of shingle that had been washed into the streets were fish, mostly dead, although a few still flapped feebly in salt puddles. The gulls reappeared and flew screaming about, now and then landing to gulp down what the sea had thrown up. Outside Granny Mundy's house a drowned horse lay with its mane plastered to the stones, its position marked by an outline of sand the retreating currents had drawn. Martin and Will were moved by how beautiful it was, how the hooves curled at a trot, how the tail was spread like unraveled silk over the cobbles, the wet flanks gleaming the color of polished chestnut. It might have been asleep but for the bloom on its eyes and the silt in its nostrils.

The townfolk moved unhurriedly about. There was little talk. Now and again somebody weeping would be escorted into a house and occasionally one of the fishermen searching a ruined cottage would give a cry. The town echoed to the shriek of gulls and the sound of shovels scraping against stone. Over the whole place there hung a pungent smell. It was the same smell Martin had noticed when he had first stood on the beach the previous afternoon, the smell of waves and salt, but intensified until it was almost glandular, as if the town had been overlain with the deepest and most secret parts of the sea. To this smell was added that of drying fish and weed.

On the beach a gang of fishermen found three bodies dressed in sailors' clothes. They were all foreigners.

"Frenchies," the gossip ran. "Poor damned Frenchies. Aye, the sea's no respecter of fisherfolk, whether they pray in English or in French."

But Martin had not forgotten the strange conversation he had had, and was not so mystified as many others when the body of Granny Mundy was discovered stranded in an alley and half shrouded in a bolt of purple silk.

"She can't have been a witch, after all," was all they said. "Witches don't drown, everybody knows that."

Martin said nothing. He wondered what had happened to the blond girl, Mary, but soon forgot about her.

Gradually, he and Will found their steps drawn back to the scene of their meeting. The sea had retreated, the land left licking its wounds in the thin sunlight. Where the Seneschal's House had stood was now water: the waves had bitten a piece out of the haunch of East Anglia and were now digesting it at leisure. A fresh sand cliff had formed farther inland and from it they watched in silence as the water surged peristaltically around the island of rubble. Most of the house lay beneath the surface, but by some freakish circumstance the ice-cream-cone roof of the tower poked up out of the surf in an absurd monument.

"I can't believe it," was all Will could say. "Any of it."

Martin shook his head.

"Neither can I. But what matters is that we're here."

"For how long?" asked Will sadly.

"Oh, come on," laughed Martin, although it

cost him an effort. "For as long as we like, of course."

"I wasn't thinking of that," said Will as they picked their way back to the battered town. Martin knew he wasn't.

They stopped at Mrs. Banty's again because there was nowhere else to go. By now she had a fire roaring and damp things steamed on the fire screen before it. She ladled soup for them into earthenware bowls and they sat in the hearth to drink it.

"I've got an odd feeling," said Will when he had finished his.

"What about?" asked Martin.

"Well, us, I suppose. I feel as if something has just ended instead of begun."

It was not what Martin wanted to hear at all, but he couldn't pretend he hadn't noticed the same feeling in himself.

"Me too," he admitted. "Perhaps it's anticlimax after all that excitement last night."

Will looked at him quizzically.

"Perhaps it is," he agreed. "I hope so. I think we should be friends."

It was the first time anybody had ever said that to Martin. Involuntarily, his eyes filled with tears; to shield his emotion, he bent quickly forward and took great care in setting his soup bowl down on the uneven bricks of the fireplace.

"Do you really mean that, Will?" he asked at length.

"Of course I do," said Will, wiping his mouth.

"I should think we'd make very good friends; we're alike." He yawned. "I'm so tired I can hardly sit up," he said. "I'm sure Mrs. Banty wouldn't mind if we had a bit of sleep. You must be absolutely worn out too."

Until that moment Martin hadn't even thought about sleep, but now that Will had suggested it, he found he was having difficulty focusing his eyes. When Mrs. Banty came back for the soup bowls a minute or so later, she found the boys curled up together on the hearth, fast asleep. She spread a dry blanket gently over them and let them sleep on.

7

THE FIRST THING Martin saw when he awoke was Dr. Herbert. He was standing by his bedside looking at the green folder. Martin must have made some slight noise or movement because the doctor raised his eyes and looked at him.

"Aha," he said, "back in the land of the living, are we?"

Martin waited for his inner mechanism to slam down the protective barriers and enable him to withdraw peaceably, but nothing happened. Instead of shrinking, Dr. Herbert remained uncompromisingly life-size. Not only that, but Martin found he didn't even mind; he felt extremely cheerful.

"I suppose I'm back in the Hall?" he asked, in a somewhat surprised tone.

"You certainly are in the Hall," agreed the bald young doctor, "but it's hardly surprising, considering."

Much puzzled, Martin tried to marshal his thoughts.

"But I am surprised," he confessed. "I mean, how did you find me?"

It was the doctor's turn to look puzzled.

"You were never lost, were you?" he asked, flipping his folder shut.

"Not exactly *lost*, perhaps, but . . . well, how did you know to look in Mrs. Banty's house?"

Dr. Herbert frowned at him and then took hold of his left wrist, glancing at his watch as he did so.

"It's all right, old man," he said, "you've had a dream, that's all. Nothing to worry about; you'll soon forget it. Now then, how do you feel?"

"Very well," admitted Martin, "but I don't understand what you're saying. I didn't have a dream as far as I know. I remember falling asleep in Mrs. Banty's house with Will and that's all until I woke up just now."

Dr. Herbert was beginning to look slightly impatient. He let go of Martin's wrist, picked up the folder, scribbled in it with a ball-point pen, and then said, "Believe me, Martin, I don't know a Mrs. Banty. You'll just have to take my word for it: you haven't been anywhere. You've been asleep in here for the last forty-four hours. I must say, you look a great deal better than you did when we got you to bed. You sound better, too; we couldn't get a word out of you then. Now, I suggest we get you something to eat and then you could think about getting up if you feel you can cope."

With a cheery wave, the doctor went out, shutting the door. Martin lay back, bewildered. He was definitely in the Hall. The room he was in, although not the one he shared with Ropey Dunning, was almost identical. How had he got there? Why should Dr. Herbert lie to him and pretend that he had never been outside the house? It was obviously a conspiracy. Some of his old feelings about being threatened began waking up and stretching inside him. Then the handle of the door rattled and Miss Brunt came in carrying a tray. She looked very pleased to see him.

"Martin," she exclaimed, "you look so well! Oh, I *am* glad; you must be feeling much better to look like that."

"I do feel better," agreed Martin, "but I want to know why that doctor tells me lies."

"Dr. Herbert? I don't think he'd deliberately lie to you, Martin. Why should he?"

"I don't know, but he did. He said I'd never been out of this bed in the last forty-something hours and he pretended he didn't know Mrs. Banty."

Miss Brunt set the tray gently down on the end of the bed.

"Sit up, Martin," she urged. "Have some breakfast. You can tell me as you eat." She packed pillows behind his shoulders and laid the tray across his thighs.

"But I want to know why he lied to me," protested Martin, as he buttered his toast.

"He didn't lie," said Miss Brunt, perching at

his feet. "Really he didn't. You haven't been out of this bed, honestly. I was in here most of the time and you never once woke up. You must have been dreaming."

"That's what he said."

"Well, where did you think you had been?"

"In Carisburgh, of course. I was caught there by the storm."

"Storm? Be careful, Martin," she added, "you're slopping tea on the sheet."

"The storm last night," said Martin, exasperated, but Miss Brunt was shaking her head.

"Really, there wasn't a storm. It's been rather nice, actually."

"Of course there was a storm." Martin was nearly shouting in his frustration. "How else would the sea come up and destroy thirty-one houses in Carisburgh? I was there; I watched it happening."

Miss Brunt put a hand on one of his blanket-covered feet.

"It was a dream, love, honestly. There wasn't a storm here; and in any case, there aren't thirty-one houses in Carisburgh to be knocked down. It's tiny and quite some distance from the sea as well."

Martin put down his cup. Doubts were beginning to creep into his head, like famished mice into a cheese, gnawing away at what he thought had been hard fact. It was true, there had been something strange about Carisburgh. There had been no cars there, only horses and carts. No electricity, either, come to that. Plenty of candles and lanterns, but not a light bulb anywhere. Then, as before, Granny Mundy's words came back to him as she was reminiscing about her youth . . . "The year of Our Lord, fifteen hundred and seventy, it was." And Jeremiah Howlett, what had he said about the Seneschal's House? Something about there being no reason for it to fall down in sixteen hundred. Sixteen hundred!

"I'll never see Will again," said Martin. He felt an enormous sense of loss. It was like one's tongue discovering the gap after a tooth has been extracted under local anesthetic. There was no pain, only a pulpy unevenness that he didn't want to probe and which he knew would soon hurt.

"Tell me about Will," said Miss Brunt quietly.

"Oh, he was just someone," Martin said evasively. He was still unable to believe that the events he remembered so well had taken place in his own brain.

"I'm sorry, Martin, I didn't mean to be nosy."

"No. It's all right. I'm just . . . just a bit muddled about everything. It all seemed so real."

"It usually does," agreed Miss Brunt. "But don't go thinking that because whatever it was didn't happen it therefore wasn't important."

They both sat in reflective silence while Martin finished his breakfast. He discovered that he had been very hungry. Miss Brunt watched approvingly.

"You didn't need much help with that, did

you?" she remarked. "It's the first time you've eaten that I didn't have to stand over you with a spoon."

"I feel better," said Martin simply.

"I'm very glad to hear it. Now, do you want to stay there in bed or would you like to get up? You do just what you want."

"I'll get up," said Martin. He suddenly felt energetic. He needed to walk about and think.

He dressed and they went down. Halfway down the main staircase the woman with the lily blazed out of her window in a riot of Pre-Raphael-ite shrubbery, the colors flickering across Miss Brunt's face as she passed.

"The sun's lovely today," she said. "October's often so beautiful in Suffolk."

Martin stopped and looked through the glass. The drive and the grounds outside took on strange properties. He squinted through a peony and the world was a red inferno dominated by a rogue sun that was going nova. Through a fallen autumn leaf it was a sepia photograph of an Edwardian summer. A clump of rushes took him into his familiar cool, green undersea depths. Martin was amazed at how slight a shift in his position could bring about such radical changes.

"I expect you'd like to go outside," said Miss Brunt. "You had better take a coat. It's quite nippy even though the sun is out."

At the bottom of the stairs they turned to the right.

"Where are we going?" asked Martin.

"To get your coat. The cloakroom's along here. Don't you remember?"

They stopped at a door halfway along the passage. The walls of the room inside were lined with tall tin lockers with vents in them. Each bore a name written on sticking plaster; each was painted dark green. Martin's coat was clean and dry. He shrugged it on and plunged his hands into his pockets. There was no trace of jam.

"Where's the kitchen?" he asked suddenly.

"The kitchen?" Miss Brunt sounded surprised. "Are you still hungry?"

"Oh no. I just wondered where it was, that's all."

"It's down in the basement," said Miss Brunt.

It seemed to Martin that he had dreamed a good deal.

"When did I fall asleep?" he asked, buttoning up his coat.

"We put you to bed the day before yesterday after lunch. Don't you remember any of it? We had just been to see Dr. Herbert and you said you wanted to go out for some fresh air. I watched you go out and it was just as well I did. You wobbled down those stone steps outside and fell flat on your face. You were quite ill, you know. You couldn't talk or move to do anything, so we popped you into bed and Dr. Herbert gave you some medicine. It seems to have worked."

"So I even dreamed the balloon," said Martin sadly.

"Certainly," said Miss Brunt, puzzled. "Now,

off you go and get some fresh air. I'll give you a call when it's lunchtime."

"Don't worry, I'll come back," said Martin, grinning.

From a window Dr. Herbert watched him wander about the grounds. The boy's hands were stuffed into his pockets and his head was bent but there was something about the way he was sauntering that was thoughtful rather than dejected. After a bit, his strollings took him to the gravel drive and he shortly disappeared behind the rhododendron bushes in the direction of the main gates. For fifteen minutes the bald young doctor sat on a corner of his desk and tapped his teeth with his ball-point pen, gazing vacantly out of the window. The only sounds in the room were the ticking of a clock and the clicking of this little ivory xylophone. Dr. Herbert discovered that by opening and closing his mouth he could alter the pitch of the note produced by his front teeth. Uncertainly, he tapped out "God Save the Queen" and then, more skillfully, "Abide with Me." Suddenly Martin reappeared from behind the bushes, apparently deep in thought. Dr. Herbert let out a sigh. He reached behind him and lifted the telephone receiver, still watching the boy.

"Operator? Get me London, please." He gave the number and waited, began to play "We Shall Not be Moved" on his teeth and then broke off. "Dr. Smedley? Philip, it's Tim Herbert here. We've just had the Molloney boy under narcosis and it seems to have done the trick—for the present, at any rate. I know it's early yet, but what do you want done about him? Do we hang on to him for the present and see what's what? . . . Yes . . . Yes, of course; that's true." Dr. Herbert watched Miss Brunt hurry across the lawn outside and say something to Martin. The boy turned with a smile and followed her back into the house, talking. "We'll keep him for a bit, then, Philip," said Dr. Herbert. "With any luck we should eventually be able to get him back to school with some hope of his staying there. It'll make all the difference to him. Martin's pretty lonely, although he seems to have taken quite a fancy to Nurse Brunt, which is a good thing. Better than seashells, or whatever . . . What? . . . Oh no; she's a middle-aged stick. You know, dried-up; lots of frustrated maternal instincts. She's dead keen on him . . ." Dr. Herbert laughed, shook his head once or twice, and then hung up.

After lunch Miss Brunt said to Martin, "I'm off duty this afternoon. I was going into the village for a few things; would you like to come along? We could go and look at the sea."

"Do you really want me to come?"

"Of course I do. I wouldn't have asked otherwise."

Martin put on his coat again and they walked down the drive. At the gates he chuckled.

"I came down here this morning," he said. "I walked right up to these gates." He ran his hand over the ironwork as if he needed to be convinced that it was solid; then he bent forward and sniffed it. It smelled of wet pennies. "They were open and I thought, well, what's to stop me just walking straight out again?"

"But you didn't," said Miss Brunt. It was a half question.

"No."

"Because you knew they'd start a search for you?"

"I don't know," admitted Martin. "I suppose. I only wanted to go to Carisburgh to see . . . to see how much I had dreamed about. I think I was sort of scared in case I found out that it was all crazy and unreal, though."

"Please tell me about the dream, Martin. No, don't, if you don't want to, of course, but I would like to hear it."

So Martin told her the whole story, from the finding of the balloon to the moment when he fell asleep with Will on Mrs. Banty's hearth. Miss Brunt listened in silence as they walked along. When he had finished, she asked, "Did you tell Dr. Herbert all this?"

"No." Martin shrugged. "He was too busy telling me I had been dreaming and anyway, I didn't want to."

"I can understand that. You don't like him, do you?"

"No. Well, I don't know him, do I? He doesn't seem to care much. Do you like him, Miss Brunt?"

"No," said Miss Brunt indiscreetly. "This must go no further, mind, but although I'm sure he's an excellent doctor he seems to me to be completely lacking in any sympathy." She might have been giving evidence at an inquest. "Not at all the sort of person one would wish to confide in. Poor Martin, you've had an awful time. I think you realize how important your dream was, don't you?"

"I suppose so," said Martin, frowning. "It must be, or else I wouldn't remember it all so clearly. I'm still not convinced it didn't actually happen. But it's got a meaning, hasn't it?"

"Oh yes; all dreams have meaning. You know what a computer is? Well, your mind's a bit like one, only in your case it was being fed such a great jumble of information it couldn't sort it out in time. You were all seized up, so we put you to sleep to give your poor brain a chance. While you were asleep, of course, no new information could get through into the computer and it had the opportunity to go on working quietly away at the problems you had set it while you were awake. That's why you have dreams. They often seem like nonsense only because the mind works in a sort of code made of images and pictures instead of words. Your dream was very clear, wasn't it?"

"It certainly was," said Martin. "Well, tell me what it meant."

"No," said Miss Brunt.

"Oh, go on," he urged. "I want to know. And anyway, you said it was important."

"So it is, but that doesn't mean I should tell you. The dream's clear, and you're quite capable of working it out for yourself. You think about it— that's where most of the value lies. If I explained it all you wouldn't benefit much because you wouldn't be making any effort of your own."

"Please," cried Martin.

But Miss Brunt was inflexible. "I'll give you a lead," was all she would say. "As far as I know it was the first dream you've had about people, right?"

"Yes," Martin nodded.

"No seashells?"

"No."

"So perhaps people really do matter to you, after all? Think about it. Anyway, who was Will? I think he was more than simply a friend you invented for company. Any ideas?"

Martin shook his head.

"Well," said Miss Brunt, "think how alike you and Will were. You've also been made to feel like a prisoner, haven't you? And the authorities who have been your Jeremiah Howlett have been equally well-meaning but tyrannical."

Martin had a sudden insight. "You mean the Seneschal's House was really Carisburgh Hall?" he said in a surprised voice.

"You're getting warmer," Miss Brunt nodded approvingly. "It's certainly true to say that both your lives in your respective prisons were threatened by the sea. Your dream sea came very close to winning, too, only you were also rescued just in time. The question is, who rescued *you* from your prehistoric ocean? There," said Miss Brunt in mock exasperation, "I've practically told you *every*thing . . . Oh, here we are."

Martin had hardly been noticing where they were going. He looked up and saw a handful of houses dotted around a small green. On the edge of the grass stood a telephone box and a bench.

"Where's this?" he asked.

"Carisburgh," said Miss Brunt. "Slightly different nowadays, isn't it?"

"But where's the sea?"

"That's about a quarter of a mile farther on. We'll go there in a little while. I just want to buy a couple of things first."

They went into the only shop in the hamlet, a general store, which was also a post office. Miss Brunt bought a book of stamps and a roll of Scotch tape.

"What else?" she asked aloud, looking over the crammed shelves. "Ooh, and a bottle of that pine-oil bubble bath, please." The man behind the counter made a neat package.

"What's a bubble bath?" asked Martin. The assistant smiled.

"They're great fun. You pour it into your bath and then froth it up and it'll bubble right up to the top. It helps soften the water, or something. It also makes you smell nice."

Martin, watching this gray, middle-aged woman paying for her purchases, felt a sudden pang of unbearable pity. She had stood between Dr. Herbert and himself ever since his arrival at Carisburgh Hall, and in return he wanted to take the place of the bubble-bath liquid and shield her from whatever it was that threatened her. But when they stood outside again he could find no words, so he simply took her hand in a gesture of solidarity.

The road led through the sort of countryside he had seen so vividly in his dream. The soil was sandy, with outcrops of gorse and pine trees. Soon they rounded a bend and there lay the sea. For the last time Martin wondered whether his dream hadn't really taken place after all: the resemblance of his dream landscape to the place now before them was remarkable. It was as if he had been here before, not because he recognized any particular landmark but because the general impression and atmosphere of the place so exactly matched that of the dream. The road ended in an empty sandy area, presumably used as a car park in summer. Beyond it was a guard rail and, climbing over this, they found themselves on the very edge of a crumbling sand cliff about twenty feet above a shingle beach. Miss Brunt was watching Martin as he gazed at the sea and the beach and the occasional circling gull.

"Does it look familiar?" she asked at length.

"It's fantastic," said Martin. "It does and yet it doesn't. I know I've never been here before, and it doesn't feel as if I've been here before, yet everything in the dream looked pretty much like this." He waved a hand at the scene. Despite the sunshine the sea was gray and so flat that only the occasional glint of a distant wave betrayed its movement. The surf in the foreground broke on the shingle, but somehow it didn't seem to be representative of the sea at all but merely the lunatic fringe.

"You see there are still bits of the ruins left," Miss Brunt said, pointing to the right. Among the gorse and the bushes were the remains of a flint-faced stone wall. "That's the end of Old Carisburgh, and that's why they built the new village well inland." They walked over to the wall. "This was the church that used to stand at the rear of the town," said Miss Brunt, sitting on the loose stones. "Don't go too close to the edge, but if you can just peep over you'll see that the last of the churchyard's being washed away right at this moment."

Martin peered cautiously over the edge, holding on to some gorse roots. The slope below was littered with fragments of headstones, among them sandy-colored tubes and shards like pieces of broken teacups. "There are bones down here," he called up.

"I know. Every time there's a storm the edge crumbles away a bit and some more come down. You can often find complete skulls at the bottom, teeth and all. People take them home and polish them up and stand them on top of the piano. They call them jolly names like Fred and invent lurid pasts for them, transferring all their own fantasies to them. That way they can leave themselves blameless. It makes me rather cross. The bones are just the last of Old Carisburgh's inhabitants on their way to join the others. They shouldn't be treated like dolls."

Martin had never heard Miss Brunt so indignant.

"How do you know all this?" he asked. "I mean, about people cleaning up the skulls."

"Dr. Herbert's got one," she answered shortly. "He uses it as a paperweight and talks to it; I've heard him."

Martin stood on the very edge and stared out over the water. He thought of the once great city of Carisburgh lying beneath the sea, the drowned churches and the cobbled streets thronged with fish. He knew that his own dream world lay buried there as well: the Seneschal's House, Granny Mundy's cottage, Mrs. Banty's pigsty. Only Will refused to go quietly beneath the waves. He still stood vividly in Martin's mind and the expected pain of loss still wouldn't come. After some thought Martin decided that this was because as his friend had only ever existed in his brain he was still there, if anywhere at all. It was only necessary to make the effort to recall him, but he didn't make the effort.

Miss Brunt was watching him from the rotting wall on which she sat motionlessly in her plain coat, her graying hair moved by the light breeze. Her instinct had been right; her feelings of hope on first meeting him were fully justified. This thin, dark boy would soon be sent back to London for schooling, she knew. And that was right; it was proper that he should be among children of his own age and intelligence. She wondered who would be sent to fill the gap in her endlessly replenished family. Some simple delinquent, probably; another Ropey Dunning. Sometimes she hated her job; often she hated Carisburgh with its gray sea air and the gulls making their lonely sounds.

"Shall we go?" she suggested, getting up and brushing the crumbs of mortar off her coat. "I could do with a cup of tea."

"All right." Martin turned to her and thrust his hands into his pockets. Then he drew out his left hand and looked at what he had found.

"What's that you've got?" asked Miss Brunt.

"My seashell," said Martin. It lay in his palm, a shell-shaped stone a million years dead, slightly grubby from his handling.

"Good heavens, I'd forgotten all about that," said Miss Brunt.

"So had I," admitted Martin. He gave it a last look and then threw it as far as he could into the sea. A gull screamed and dived where it hit the water in a little white splash. Deceived, the bird swooped away disgustedly.

"Nothing for you," said Martin. "You've had it." Then he took Miss Brunt's arm and they walked home.